T.F. Polte

Songogdson: The Chosen

First edition

This book was professionally typeset on Reedsy.
Find out more at reedsy.com

Contents

Acknowledgments

Mary Polte: Thank you for putting up with me for all those years talking about my ideas. Without your encouragement to "Write it down already," this story would never have proceeded past the Preface.

Ethan and Jordan Polte: Thank you for designing the cover.

Sandy Hanula: This book would never have been completed without your encouragement and assistance. You kept me focused and provided great insight. Your excitement for the next chapter to read and edit pulled me through the moments I had lost my way in the narrative. You are the reason I was able to bring this story to a close.

Brent Warren: Thank you for permission to include your personal electromagnetic pulse gun.

Jacob McElligott – Lame Horse Publishing: Thank you for taking a chance on this dream.

Prologue

The wind was blowing down from the top of the mountains, too cold for this time of year. The stallion was pacing back and forth. He turned and looked towards the mountains, searching for any sign of the danger he sensed. He got caught up in the nervousness that was infecting the entire herd, his herd. He felt that he should be protecting them but, at the same time, was being drawn away. He didn't understand it. He just had to go. He turned to one of his sons, the one he was going to send out this morning. He neighed and whinnied, then turned and ran. His son watched him go. The young stallion didn't understand why but the herd now turned to him to lead them away from this strange place. He was now the leader; he would have to earn it later, but there was no question for this moment. He turned with a final scream, leading the herd away from the strange wind—to the plains where life would return to normal.

Still confused and nervous, the old stallion followed that wind to its source. He climbed up the mountain, higher than any other horse had ever gone. Along the way, he cropped the grass growing there, not from hunger but more to comfort himself. Just the act of eating eased the stress. He found a stream and drank his thirst away. Darkness was falling, so he stayed there by the stream. He did not sleep well, waking with a start at each sound. At first light, he looked down the mountain and saw what appeared to be his herd moving out onto the plains. He desired to go after them and even started back that way, only to stop in his tracks after a few paces. He turned back up the mountain. The urge to complete the climb was still pulling him on. The path was clear to him; he could not resist following. The climb was more difficult that day. The way was steeper, and he was less sure-footed on the loose rocks. About the middle of the second afternoon, he broke into a calm clearing near a cave opening. He knew this was the place he was meant to find. He paused, looked around, and found a spring from which to take a drink. There was grass to graze on, too. He did so. He was still nervous—jumping at every sound—but found that he could not leave. Soon he noticed the sounds from inside the cave: the sounds of death. Terror nearly overwhelmed him. And yet he remained, transfixed.

The sounds eventually changed from death to something more soothing. The stallion was able to relax. The next sound he heard from the cave was a rattling as if sticks were knocking together. A whirling wind came next, starting from the clearing and moving into the cave.

Inside the cave, the sounds grew louder. The great wind sent bones scattering on jets of air coming up from deep within. The wind deposited the bones, one by one, on a ledge. As if under their own command, they formed a skeleton, one hand up behind his head in light rest. The whirlwind carried plumes of dust next, dropping it in piles over the bones. As it settled, it formed a body around the skeleton, first taking the shape of organs, muscle, skin, and clothing. It was a man. He was lean, and though age sat heavily upon him, he looked strong. However, there was no life in him. There was no movement at all except for his hair and clothes being disturbed by the breeze.

Soon the wind was devoid of dust and whirled towards the body that now lay there. It entered through the mouth and nostrils, filling the lungs. The body began to stir. It took a deep breath, coughed once, then sat up, turned, and stretched. He stood slowly and looked around, getting his bearings. The Man was tall, well over six feet, and though he looked rough, he moved with a grace and ease that belied the years marked on his face. The look in his gray-blue eyes would turn a brave man's blood cold. He looked around the cave, thinking to himself:

'How long?'

The empty space did not answer him.

He turned his head, looking from the bed, and looked towards another shelf cut into the rock wall. There, just as they had always been, were his weapons: Twin Colt 45 revolvers in a simple holster rig that held one gun at his left hip and the other at his waist just below his navel. There was also a pair of Remington revolvers with a fancy rig that would hold one at his right hip and the other at his ribs on his right side, where he could reach it easily with his left hand. The holsters held ammo for all four guns and a pack filled with casings, lead, and gunpowder to make more. Some other weapons were left from his predecessor: a knife, a longbow, and a quiver of 24 arrows. These were not always there. But apparently, he would need them this visit. He took another deep breath knowing the air to be stale, but he was just enjoying the act of breathing after so long.

"How long?" His voice was a deep rasp. Still, the cave did not answer him.

He stood, stretching out his legs, and reached out for his long coat that was hanging—as he had left it—next to the cave mouth amongst a tangle of protruding roots. When he touched the coat, the tendrils moved aside and released their treasure. He shook it out and put it on. He then strapped on his gun-belt and looped the rig with the Remington pistols across his shoulder. He checked the angle of each, ensuring he could access them all in moments. When he was satisfied, he attached a sheath and knife to his belt, then picked up the quiver and bow, looked around the cave again, and stepped into the cave shaft heading towards the light. There he found the opening carved into the side of the tunnel halfway through the shaft. It was hidden from all except those who knew where to look. He reached in and found the saddle right where he left it. Again the roots moved aside as he pulled it out. He sat on a rock and cleaned the saddle with the old rags he had left beneath it. Within no time, it shone like new, despite so many years in the elements. He then stood, picked up the saddle and his deadly possessions, and stepped out into the fresh air. The horse was there, waiting just like always—wild-eyed and terrified, prancing back and forth. It was lighter in color than he remembered, but the markings were the same. His old horse, reborn again into the body of this stallion, great, great-grandson to his own.

The man looked around the clearing, breathed deeply of the fresh air, put on his hat, and smiled. He knelt by the stream, scooped water in his hands, and drank it down. He strode to the horse, whistling a soft tune. He patted its nose cautiously, easing much of its fear with that gentle touch. The horse found the touch familiar and knew he had found his master. The man put the harness on the horse and inserted the bit. The metal bit had a strange flavor but was not painful. The horse seemed to remember the feeling from deep in the recesses of memories that didn't seem to be his own. The man then placed the blanket and saddle on his back. He tightened the straps, mumbling soothing words all the while. The saddle felt intensely familiar. When the man mounted, the horse shied for a moment or two. The urge to buck was strong, but the man was gentle and spoke in soothing tones. The horse calmed down. Then the man pulled the reins gently, urging him out through the trees. As they rode away, the cave mouth closed behind them, leaving no trace it was there. The spring feeding the stream slowed to a trickle and stopped. Horse and rider left going the way the wind told them. Something called out to both of them: someone needed their help.

1

The Choice

As he rode out of the mountain, the Man thought again about how this had started. His predecessor, the Irishman, had told him the legend from the beginning. The tale of how he had been Chosen. He remembered those words well:

"You won't be rememberin' your own name by the time ya finish with this. I been serving a long time now; too many names to remember my own. Maybe you be different. But from the beginnin, it's been this way. Started with the first Chosen, way back. The Huns had been building up again. They were to make another run at it hoping to be like Attila. They started raiding villages along their borders, taking many slaves. The leader took one lad for his own. He took the lad as an infant to replace his son, who had died at birth. He burned the lad's skin on his face to prevent the beard from growing as they did back then. He then treated the burns and took the child to his woman so she could nurse him. The lad grew in that place as the son of that cruel man. He had been named Songogdson, The Chosen because his father had selected him from the other children. He never fit in completely; he was a head taller

than any other in the camp and loads stronger. He became second only to his father as a warrior. He was destined to be a leader. The others in the band did not respect him as much as fear him. He was always an outsider, but at the same time, he was in charge. His father sent him to lead a raiding party across the border, taking gold and food from the border villages. His attacks were legendary. He left no one alive who could later return to harm him.

As he came to the last village, one of the older raiders told him that it was his birthplace. He listened to the story from his men, how he had been taken from here. He asked if anyone was left alive at that time. The men replied that only the older men and women were left here. The old men were too feeble to take as slaves and most of the women had been used and tortured; none had been expected to live through that winter. His men said that others must have rebuilt the village. He led the attack the following day and found himself in the middle of the town supervising the destruction his men wrought. He turned to find himself facing an older woman with a bow drawn. She would have killed him if she had let the arrow fly.

He turned fully to her as he threw his knife, only to notice her eyes after the blade had left his hands. He leaped from his horse and caught her as she fell. He looked into her eyes, eyes that seemed so like his own. He realized then that he had killed his own mother. Though he did not know her she had known him and had spared him. She could have killed him but had stopped and waited for him to turn. His thoughts returned to his men and what they were doing. He turned on them. He began to kill them one at a time until they finally realized what was happening. In his rage, he took them all on and took their lives. In this act, he saved the village, but he was fatally injured and lay dying in a puddle of his own blood. He turned to the remaining villagers and used what few simple signs and words of their language he knew to tell them who he was. He told them that he was not worthy of returning to them. With the last of his strength, he rose and fell upon his own sword. He collapsed there, before a shrine to their God in the center of the village. As he faded into death, an old man, the village's holy man, came to him. The stranger issued a prayer, his voice at once deep and quiet. The righteous man looked into his eyes as he prayed. He spoke for all to hear:

"This warrior has been returned to us by the Gods to save us from this evil.
Now he is returned to them.
They will provide his protection for all time to those in need."

The warrior heard the holy man's voice. As the old man spoke, his voice seemed to change from one to many. There were many telling him he could refuse, but he seemed unable to reply. He knew this was his path. The voices, one by one, changed into a terrible chant that rang in his ears. He knew he should be dead but was unable to leave his body. He was trapped in this place between life and death, waiting for the call. His name was Songogdson; he accepted his fate. He was the first Chosen and knew this would be his curse till he had paid for his sins. He faded into the deep sleep that should have been the release of death. But he did not receive that release. He remained, not alive, not dead, no sensation; only a feeling of timelessness and waiting."

The Irishman had told him this, and the Man knew it was true. It was similar to what had happened to him. He had been working for the railroad; they took towns and farmland with force when necessary. He had only involved himself in purchasing the lands from the willing sellers. Soon enough, he discovered why they were ready to sell. He learned the railroad had hired men to terrorize the people till they had no other choice.

The railroad men were ruthless, drunk on their power. He witnessed several men beaten nearly to death and some who the rail workers shot where they stood. No one could stand before these butchers. One among the townsfolk was different: a big Irishman giving the railroad men all they could handle. He admired the man's courage and wished he could aid his cause.

The next evening, he had his opportunity when the workers requested he go with them to the last farmer's land. When he arrived, the farmer was already bruised and bleeding from the beating he had taken. Still, he refused to leave his land.

The railroad men dragged the farmer's wife and daughters out of the house and held them within sight of the farmer, threatening them with their weapons. The Irishman appeared behind the two men holding the women and killed them both with his bare hands before they realized someone was upon them.

When he was finished, the Irishman led the women away, defending them with his Remington guns till he ran out of ammo. They were trapped there by the three remaining railroad men. Pinned by gunfire, they had no choice but to surrender.

The women were pulled away and tied to the fence, and the railroad men opened fire on the Irishman. As the Irishman was being killed before him, the Man could take no more. He stepped up, pulled his guns, and killed the three railroad men. Because of his bastard boss and his men, too many had died.

So with cold eyes, no longer a railroad man, he stood up to them for the farmer's family and the big Irishman. Too late, perhaps, but soon enough to save this family. He took them back inside the house when it was done and made sure they were safe. Then he returned to his horse and mounted up. As he rode away, he didn't see the big Irishman sitting up, gravely wounded but still alive.

The Irishman watched the railroad man leave. His breathing was growing stronger by the second. The blood flow from his wounds slowed and then stopped as the holes scared over. The look in the Irishman's eyes was hopeful. He pulled himself to his feet, checked on the family, and left them to care for each other. The wife offered to tend his wounds, but he stopped her as she opened his shirt. He saw the confusion followed by fear on her face when she saw that the holes had already scarred over. He asked her quietly to keep his secret then mounted his horse and rode after the railroad man.

The former railroad man cursed himself.

'I should have never taken this job.'

The Man was on a path he could not turn from now. He rode back to town to confront his employer. The only way he could pay compensation for the sins he had committed.

He entered the village to many suspicious glances from the townspeople. No one would look in his eyes, which were far too cold. He dismounted in the street, not stopping to tie his horse. He slapped the haunch and watched as the horse trotted off a few paces, stopped, and turned back to look at him. The Man then turned, entered the railroad field headquarters, and stormed into the office. He was met by his employer and a couple of executives.

They all had their men there, but he didn't care. He interrupted their meeting with his accusations and demanded that they call off the attacks. His arguments were loud, and people in the street outside could hear it all. Then they listened to the first shots and the rapid staccato of a quick gunfight fight.

The Man killed them all coldly and with superior skill, but they outnumbered him greatly, and several of their shots had struck him in the frenzy.

He stumbled back out of the front door, covered in blood, and whistled for his horse. Wounds dripping, he mounted up and rode out of town. He knew he would never get far—these wounds were surely mortal.

The horse chose their direction as the Man faded out of consciousness.

The Man heard the strange voices, imploring him to choose. They did not tell him his options, but he knew one choice must be death—the fate he knew he deserved yet found he did not want to take.

"The other choice then," he murmured as he slumped down in the saddle. The voices rose to a crescendo, louder even than gunfire. Unable to stop, he slipped from the saddle.

He awoke in the Irishman's arms. Somehow, they were farther outside of town than he had ridden. The Irishman was tending his wounds and talking, telling the stories of the Chosen. The last was about a cave that would be their refuge. The Irishman spoke of the choice that the Man had made. A choice he had not recognized the truth of when he had made it.

He felt that his act was his choice, but he was now chosen

regardless of how. He marveled at his new scars. They looked years old, even though he knew they happened in the last several hours. The two men mounted their horses again and left that place. They rode an old trail towards the mountains. The Irishman told him more of the stories as he took him to the cave and how the shelter opened where needed. He could be in a different land, a foreign country, but he would always be where he had to be. He would always have help if needed. As the Irishman spoke, they rode high into the mountain. The few times he looked behind him, he saw that they had somehow left behind no trail—as if they had not passed this way at all. They finally came to a small clearing with a jagged cave opening surrounded by roots. They dismounted and removed the saddles and bridles from their horses.

The Irishman slapped his horse on the rump, and it trotted away.

"Be free, old friend," he said. They watched the horse stride away.

The Irishman gestured towards the cave and spoke:

"After you."

As the railroad man entered the cave, a rustling wind sounded behind him as if a pile of sticks had fallen over. When he turned back to the opening, he found only a pile of bones so old that they turned to dust and blew away when the wind blew. He saw the Irishman's saddle and weapons on a rock shelf. They looked as if they had been there for years. Roots of vines had grown around them. He laid his guns down on the shelf next to them. Tree roots immediately surrounded them. He hung his saddle on a rock in the chamber across the opening; the roots also covered it. He hung his long coat by the tree root and walked out to his horse. The Irishman's horse was gone. He removed the bridle and smoothed out the mane, the beast would be free now. He turned the horse towards the plains below and slapped its rear. It stepped from the clearing, turned back, and shook its head. The man and the clearing were gone. The trees were closing in behind him. One direction the horse could go, so it turned and trotted down the mountainside towards the plains. He spotted the wild horses there and was filled with the desire to take this herd. He would challenge for leadership and make this herd his own.

The man had stepped back into the cave. He wrapped the bridle in the blanket and placed them with the saddle. Satisfied they were secure, he turned into the cave and lay down on the rock bed. He began to feel tired. He rubbed his hand over the scars left by the bullets; "Bullets that should have killed me," he thought as he drifted off to sleep. As he slept, his breathing slowed and then stopped. His heart stopped. The cave mouth had closed. He was suddenly aware that he could not breathe and yet knew he would remain here, unable to leave his body even as it turned to dust.

2

Annie

The house was quiet, but that was not unusual now. The mother sighed as she realized, not for the first time, that the kids were getting too old to be playing loud. Sometimes she missed it. She was not sure whether her some was even home at that point. She settled with her daughter in front of the TV for the evening,

"Where's Dad?" the young girl asked.

"He's working late again," her mother replied.

She still worried that her father would be found out and they would all be moving again. He had been a critical witness in a criminal trial. He had to, because her brother had hacked into the wrong computers and had found out just what their father's associates had been up to.

Their father had turned himself in and had agreed to testify for the protection of his family. His testimony had taken down several executives and politicians who had been involved. Through his statements and the information her brother had uncovered, they flushed out several group members, but not all of them. For their protection, they had been given new names and identities. It had been four years now. It was a difficult change, but things were beginning to settle now.

She turned back to the TV. She was almost sixteen years old now and was starting to watch fewer comedy shows. She felt she was getting too old for the childish humor. This evening she was watching a show about ancient mysteries. She did not know the program's name but had been thoroughly absorbed in the stories it told. They spoke of different ancient legends, and the host attempted to prove that there was an objective factual basis in history for them.

The show was returning after a newsbreak to the narrator in mid-sentence, "—is the Songogdson. He was a warrior who turned from evil through selfless acts of rescue, restoration, or revenge for the helpless, to become the savior of the downtrodden, usually at the loss of his mortal life. The story is that in dark times he comes to those in need. He has been a re-occurring legend throughout ancient times and even more recent incidents in some western legends from only 200 years ago. This man is said to be the Chosen, bound to help humanity in times of need."

There was a grainy photograph from an early camera. The only thing in focus was the eyes of a man. They were gray and cold and seemed to stare back out of the photo. It was frightening to look into that face. He had the look of someone who could kill without conscience or hesitation. She thought about him for a long time, asking questions of herself that she could not answer.

Could this truly happen? Where could a guy like that go today?

Her mother's voice penetrated the drone of the TV:

"Annie!"

"What is it?" she called back, embarrassed that she hadn't

heard her mom calling.

"Where is Thomas tonight?"

"Tommy? He's out with Sarah at the mall again."

"Well, he left the basement door open outside and forgot to take the saw back out to the shed."

Her mother paused, and Annie knew what was coming and was already heading to the basement stairs before her mother even asked her to. Knowing Tommy, he probably had not even cleaned up after himself after working on building his new shelf. She figured she would probably end up having to clean up after him, as usual.

3

Tom

The mall was crowded, but that did not bother Thomas. He felt more comfortable in a crowd than hiding out alone. He had made a game of it, hiding from the mall cops and shoplifting what he could without getting caught. It was a way to entertain himself after his computer privileges had been taken away. He had been caught hacking into different systems three times, and they had been forced to move and change identities again. So he entertained himself with petty theft instead.

Today, however, he was with Sarah Abraham, the most wonderful girl he had ever known. Nothing could deter him from being the gentleman she deserved. He knew he would never live up to her family's standards, but she liked him and would go out with him whenever he asked. Always as a friend, though he wished for more.

They walked by a street vendor on their way back to the car when the vendor called out to them:

"Fortunes read, your future seen, come into my stall, and you will know all about the next few weeks, months, or years." They looked over and saw an old woman. Her sign read *Miss*

Maribel - Clairvoyant, Medium.

"Let's give her a try," Sarah said. Tom nodded and laughed. To please her, he would do anything. He did not believe in this stuff but was willing to listen for her sake.

Sarah paid the lady and sat down in the chair. The old medium reached out and gently took Sarah's hand and turned it up, so her palm was facing the fortune teller.

She frowned, peering hard at Sarah's hand. "Difficult trouble ahead; you have found true love without knowing. There will be struggles; family you will lose and, more importantly, family you will gain." She paused, pursing her lips. "There is more in your future that will be painful, but long life is yours, and you will find true love and happiness returned to you after the pain and struggle."

Then she turned to Thomas. He looked at Sarah and shrugged; he could see that the reading disturbed her. The old lady was still looking at him.

Sarah smiled at him and giggled. "Your turn. I paid her for two; now sit down."

He sat and looked at the woman. She took his hand and held it firmly, looking into his palm. The old woman began to tremble and tried at first to step back from her table. A force seemed to stop her, holding her in place. Her face was awash with fear, and she trembled as she cried out.

"Go to your home now!" she said. "I know not what it means, but I get the vision of someone saying your father has been 'found out.'"

Thomas did not hesitate; he turned to Sarah, who looked back in shocked concern. "I have to check on something. Could you wait here?"

He kissed her, then. She stared at him, surprised by the kiss.

He looked into her eyes. "If anyone comes looking for you, stay hidden!"

He stepped to the front of the stall and looked out. There were two men he recognized from the trial in which his father had testified. It looked as though they had just walked by in the direction of his car.

He knew what this meant; they were in big trouble. The old woman was trembling and saying a prayer in a strange language. Suddenly she switched to English:

"Chosen, please come to help this family. They are in great need of your protection. I pray that you do not come too late." She turned to Tom. "Go out this way, get home quick. The police will already be there. Don't worry about the girl. I will keep her safe till this danger is passed."

He hesitated a moment, not sure he could trust the old woman, but seeing he had no choice, he left out the back as she commanded. He arrived at home several minutes later to find his father lying on the driveway surrounded by police. The house was open and surrounded by yellow tapes declaring *Police Line Do Not Cross.* Thomas pushed to the front and under the tape. He was intercepted by a dark-skinned man in a black overcoat. The man held him back with a firm hand on his chest and introduced himself as agent Johnston from the Federal Witness relocation program. As he informed Tom about his father and mother's death, Tom could barely register what he said. They were killed along with a neighbor who had been outside and came to investigate the noises. His sister was missing.

"I saw them at the mall," Tom said.

"Who did you see?" the officer replied.

"I saw two men who were in the paper when Dad testified.

They were some of the ones who got off without charges. I can't remember their names."

Tom looked over his shoulder as he spoke and saw the neighbor being carted into the hearse by a pair of people in white uniforms. He then saw a black car moving up slowly towards him. The back door opened and Johnston asked him to enter. He turned to the man and noticed his gun was not in his holster.

Tom could not see the weapon from where he stood but knew it had to be pointed at him somehow. He turned back to the car and entered the open door. He slid across to the opposite side and noticed there was no door handle—no escape. He turned in his seat to watch the officer enter the car after him.

"You are one difficult kid to track down, son," said Johnston.

"What do you mean?" Tom asked. He noticed the gun had found its way back into the holster.

"Well, we knew you were found out, but we were too late to get here in time. We know you are familiar with what your father had worked on in the case, and we need you now to help us get the people who did this. Either that or you get charged with the crime."

"You can't do that! I have witnesses as to where I was all night."

"If they survived," the man said. "You saw the other men at the mall. You said so yourself."

Tom shuddered. He began a silent prayer for Sarah as he turned and looked out the window.

"Where's my sister?" he said finally.

"Was she at home tonight? We didn't find her body or any trace of a struggle. Could she have been out visiting someone?"

the man asked.

"Not unless mom and dad changed their minds about that party." He paused, remembering their conversation. "They said she was too young to be going to an all-night party at a friend's house."

The man got on the radio. "Dispatch."

"Go ahead," was the reply.

"I need you to continue the search of the surrounding area. The girl was supposed to be home tonight, but it's possible she was out at a friend's. We need to find her."

"Roger, I'll inform the search parties."

The man turned his radio down so they wouldn't be listening to the broadcast messages. Tom stayed silent for the rest of the trip.

4

Run

Annie was still running—but slower now than she would like. She was still able to hear the man chasing her. She had been hanging up the tools that Tom had left out when she saw her father pull up. He climbed out of the car and turned to the road. She heard him scream:

"Oh, God! NO!"

Then she heard the thumps of the bullets hitting the car. The silencers had kept the gun reports from being too explosively loud, but unlike movies, the noise still carried to the backyard. She slid back into the shed and glanced out at the cellar door. *No good, she thought. I locked it so Tom would have to come in the front door.* She stayed out of sight for a few seconds and then slipped out into the shadows of the backyard. She saw her Mom screaming in the kitchen but couldn't hear her until the glass blasted out alongside a spray of bullets. She turned, slipped out the gate behind the fire pit, ran, and had been running since.

She knew these trails well. She had been walking them since they moved in. Now she had been using them to hide her path, running and circling the loopback trails as much as she dared, hoping to throw off any attackers. The sound of the man in pursuit would come close at times but then fall back for a time till he figured out the false trails she left. She had seen that in a movie and hoped it would work, but in the end, she was tiring faster than her pursuer. She caught sight of him once, a rough-looking man carrying a gun. Had he been looking up instead of down at the trail, he would have seen her. He took the false path she had left, and she decided it was time to forget leaving false trails and turned back towards the mountain.

She was soon farther than she had ever been before. She was exhausted when she broke out of the woods on a small mountain road. She saw it was paved and ran offset to her trail. She was nearly 100 yards down when she turned to try to jump into the ditch over the soft dirt that would have revealed her footprints. When she looked back, she saw the man step out of the woods and look down at her. She jumped only to miss her footing on the other side. She slipped into the small ditch, and that was enough time for the man to catch up to her. He had put his gun away and dragged her back onto the road by her shirt. He pulled out a small radio in one hand.

"This is Mac. I found her!" he said. "Do we still need her?" There was a crackle over the radio, and a voice came back.

"You know the job; take her and rendezvous at the drop-off in two hours. Watch out for the Feds. They are looking for her too."

The man put the radio back in his pack and looked down at her. "Well, you heard him." He said. "Now he said I have to kill you, but he didn't say how, so I guess I can have a little fun now."

"She screamed then, and he hit her across the face, knocking her down. Just as he was reaching for her again, she heard the horse. He grabbed her arm and turned around, pulling her up and holding her between the uninvited guest and his body. The man on the horse looked at him with the ferocity of a caged lion. The younger man leveled his gun at Annie's shoulder, where the man on the horse couldn't see. "Just move along, old man. You never seen a domestic dispute before?" The rider shrugged, then went down the road a short way and down a trail into the forest.

"Smart man," her captor said into her ear as he re-holstered his gun. Now let's see how much fun you are."

He turned her around and dragged her off into the trees to a small clearing so they could no longer see the road. He strapped her arms to a tree above her head. As he started tearing at her shirt, he stiffened, stood straight, and turned around. She saw the arrow sticking from his back as he fell to the ground.

The horseman came from the woods opposite the tree she was tied to and walked across the clearing to untie her. As he came over, his horse came back up the path towards them. The man lifted her onto his horse and walked over to the dying man. He kicked the man's gun away and looked at him. Then he roughly pulled the arrow out and cleaned it off on the man's shirt.

"I wasn't really gonna kill her." The dying man groaned in pain, coughed, and was still.

The older man looked down on him:

"Well, you said you was, so now you're done."

The old man shoved the arrow back into his quiver.

He looked up at the woman with squinted eyes. "Just sit tight while I clean up this mess." He turned to his mount. "Horse, keep her safe."

The old man grabbed the dead man's collar and dragged him back up into the trees. He left him there in a shallow washout where he would not be seen right away. Then the man came back and jumped up behind her. He didn't speak as they rode for half a mile. He took her to a small cave where there was an old bedroll. He spoke with a low voice full of gravel; told her to lie down on his blanket and rest. He said he would take her to a cabin soon, but resting while he cared for his horse was better. She could not argue with him and just before she fell asleep, she realized she was looking into the eyes from the photo on the TV. He was the man in the one-hundred-year-old photo. He was the Chosen.

5

The Escape Caleb

The room was dark, as was the rest of the safe house. Thomas was shoved into the room, and the door was locked behind him. He didn't like how this was going down, but he had no way to defend himself. He glanced at the windows hoping for an escape route. There was a padlock on each one, and the windows were tinted so dark he could not see out. As his gaze circled the room, he saw a glint of reflected light and knew he was being watched. The camera would have remained hidden if not for that slight reflection.

He walked around the room, looking at the windows with his back to where he believed the camera to be. As he went by the desk, he snagged the paperweight. Keeping it hidden from the camera, he continued searching the windows. He found the light on the last window when a car came around the corner; its headlights shined through a small opening in the tint. He could just see out that opening but not enough to tell where he was. He turned to face the camera without looking directly at it. He heard another car coming and thought this would be his only chance. When the light flashed through and reflected off the camera lens, he launched the paperweight; it hit squarely on the spot of the camera reflection. He then elbowed the window, shattering it, and leaped out through the broken glass to land in a bush on the other side. He rolled over, ran to the front of the house, and ducked behind the bushes. The pursuit out the door was instantaneous, and he knew they had assumed he would immediately bolt for the woods. He watched as the bulk of the search party went there to search. He knew they wouldn't be there long, so he crept back to the window and crawled back in. He went to the door and found it was open, as he had expected. He looked into the hallway. There were no guards, and he crept to the next room. He looked in and found what he was looking for. He stepped in and sat at the desk. He turned to the keyboard and opened the internet connection. He typed in the IP address he had memorized and was rewarded with the login screen. He was surprised the server addresses were still the same. He entered the login and password. He then typed his message and hit the encrypted code. The page disappeared and wiped itself from the system. No evidence that it had been used remained.

There was a gun on the desk beside the keyboard. He slowly picked it up and quietly stepped from the desk to the entrance. He listened at the door to make sure no one was there. Satisfied the way was clear, he slowly opened the door and crept down the hall to the next door. He found it was unlocked and slipped inside to wait.

He didn't wait too long. The men were returning to the house.

"No trace of him at the forest line. No tracks." One of them reported.

"Go back out and look again. I will wait here." Tom

recognized Johnston's voice.

He stayed in the corner while Johnston started looking through the house again. Soon he stepped into the room and was waiting for his eyes to adjust.

When he saw Tom sitting there, he was startled.

"Shit! What the fuck did you think you were doing?" he snarled.

When Tom didn't move, he paused. For a moment, it seemed as if Thomas was dead. Then he saw he was breathing. He grabbed him by the arm and dragged him to his feet. He held Tom up to his face and glared into his eyes.

"You little shit! Don't you know that we are the only ones who can keep you alive?" Johnston pushed him back into a chair and continued. "These men were not involved in any of those cases before your father's trial. I chose them myself for this to keep them from being corruptible." They don't even know what this is about or who is looking for you."

Tom waited for the agent to stop and said, "Yes, I know who you are and why you are here. My dad trusted you alone. And I do too, for now. Otherwise, you would not have found me back here." I just needed to make sure you were still on my family's side, Mr. Johnston."

Johnston looked at him closely. "So what did you find out with your little venture?"

"I learned that you still keep my identity closed off from the men guarding me, so you still don't trust them." He said, "And that you still care to keep your charges alive and safe and that you still don't know who turned out my family's location. You should check the computer there in about 15 minutes to get a little information that may help you but do it when no one else is in the room or looking in on those extra cameras in there."

Agent Johnston was angry but impressed. "You have some skills, son, but next time you should think a little longer before you expose the safe house to possible public notice." He looked at Tom closely and said, "What am I going to see?"

"I am not sure, but I know how to use the password that your man left on the screen. I just accessed the phone records from your office. I turned the search to look for something not related to my dad but our phone number. I was looking for anything related to a non-secure line. Check them for any calls to my home. You turn up any calls, then check my dad's record for who called him at that time." Tom looked at him with a shrug. "If that helps you, then you tell me if Sarah is safe."

Johnston looked back at him with a stern look but one filled with more respect. He had to admit that it was a good move. "Good enough," He said. "Now we have to get you cuffed up and locked in a different room before they get back. I still don't trust all of them." He shrugged his shoulder towards the door indicating the men searching the grounds.

Tom let himself be cuffed and placed in the attic away from the other men. Johnston called on the radio for his men to come back in. When they had assembled, he told them he would stay here if the boy came to his senses and returned to the house. He sent the men out to comb the area. He said not to return to the place unless they found him. He would be available on his radio if they did find him; they should call him immediately but not to apprehend him. He would handle that himself.

After the men dispersed, he stepped back into the house

to wait at the computer. He watched the monitors from the cameras outside to ensure none of the men were hanging around. He saw no evidence of them. He did not take that for granted though and after a while switched them over to infrared for a moment. He checked camera by camera. On the second to last camera, he detected a heat source close to the edge of the woods. He flipped back to that camera and watched. A man was sitting up in the tree line just out of sight of the house. He observed the man till he walked away.

Johnston then checked the last camera and had to switch it back off of infrared due to the closeness of yet another man—so close that he was overwhelming the sensor. He was not moving but was just standing there. He was looking at the back of the man's head but could tell who it was. He had seen the man before. The odd scar in the middle of his bald spot gave him away. He was in and out of the main office lately but never seemed to be assigned to anything. He was rumored to be internal affairs, but no one really knew what department he worked for. Johnston had kept him away from this case, never revealing anything. When the man in the woods left, this man slipped away, following his men as they searched for the boy. He keyed his radio once, waited a moment, then keyed it twice more. He didn't speak, but he knew his men would be on alert now. He was watching the intruder go when the computer beep startled him. He looked back at the screen. It was a long list. He settled in to begin but left the monitors on scan to scroll at random through the cameras so he could keep a watch on the outside while he worked. When the list was fully downloaded he disconnected the line to prevent anyone prying into his work. He figured why wait and started the search immediately for the number.

It showed up twice from the payphone lines in the front of his office and once from the reception desk. He noted the dates of these calls and then deleted the file and the cache from the explorer. He then reconnected the cable modem lines and connected them back to the secure line. He called up the phone records from the home and disconnected again when he had the records for all calls from a month before to the night of the incident. He then cross-referenced the dates from the other record. There he found the match. The times and dates of the call matched up. Someone had given them up by calling on non-secure lines. He also noted the time each call took. All of them were just long enough for a tap to trace the address of the phone numbers. He now knew where to look. He could check the video of the front counter and the payphones. He had access to the tapes from his office. He also had access to the tapes from the cameras that the members of his office did not know about. He would have to cross-reference them.

The movement on the monitor had escaped his notice for too long. Now it caught his eye, but he could tell that he would be unable to get out safely with the boy. He counted three men closing in from the back and sides of the house. The only open route was out the front door, an obvious trap. He would not go that way regardless. He had just decided to let the boy loose and go out himself to try to open a pathway when one of the men dropped to his knees, then fell over obviously dead. There had been no sound. He looked back at the other monitors and saw a flash of reflected light as an arrow passed through the neck of the man at the back of the house. That left one man. Who was out there was hard to tell. No one showed on the monitors. He judged the direction of the arrow and figured the archer was somewhere by the southwest corner of the house. He made his decision to place himself between the boy and any attack. He knew what to do. He pulled an electromagnet from his briefcase and plugged it in. He held it against the PC and turned it on. Within seconds the drive was wiped completely and the system bios corrupted. The PC would reveal nothing. He went up the stairs and found the door to the room open. The boy was up and the cuffs were off. He held an old gun towards the door. He dropped it when he saw who it was.

"What took you so long?" the boy asked.

"Well, I was checking out the records as you asked. I did find something that will have to be checked out. Where did you get the gun?" Johnston asked.

"From the old man," he said.

"What old man?"

"The one out there taking out the hitmen. He said to wait till he calls, then we will leave. He also said he has my sister, and she is safe."

"Who, the hell, is he? And how the hell did he get up here and back out there?"

"I don't give a crap, as long as he is on our side...He said he saved Annie but didn't have time to tell me where he found her or even who he is."

There was a sound at the bottom of the stairs. They first heard the footsteps, then the man quietly calling for his partners, obviously knowing something was wrong but not knowing he was about to die. They heard him start up the stairs, and they pointed their weapons at the open doorway, waiting for the first sight of the intruder. Then they listened to the hum of the bow and the whoosh of an arrow, then the sound of the body falling down the stairs. After a short time, they heard the gruff voice calling, "Boy? You come on down here. If you still have that marshal there, bring him along. We gotta get moving now before the others show up."

Johnston looked to Tom and asked, "Others?"

Tom looked back and said, "We better go then."

The old man was at the door watching the tree line. He held his bow draped over one shoulder while he was cleaning the blood off of his arrows. He was replacing them into his quiver as he cleaned them. He turned and glanced at them. "They will be here soon; let's get to the trees over there and get going. Do you ride?"

"Yes," Johnston answered, unsure why but he felt the man was speaking of horses.

Tom hesitated and asked the question, "horses?"

The old man nodded

"I guess I do tonight," Tom said.

They left one at a time keeping to the shadows, the old man followed by Tom with Johnston pulling up the rear. They reached the tree line with no incident. Johnston paused and looked back at the house just before he was out of sight and saw the movement in the opposite trees. They did not see him, but he saw them. Two were his own men being led back at gunpoint. The other three included the man that he had kept removed from this case. He now knew he was right, but it still did not sit well with him. He knew his other men were giving their lives to protect their charge. It was their job; they would do it but at the hands of a colleague? His anger nearly burst his control. He had his weapon drawn and was ready to pull the trigger. He knew he was too far away to affect the outcome other than alerting everyone to where he was. He reluctantly holstered his gun and turned away to follow the old man to the break in the trees. They quietly mounted the horses. Where they came from, he did not know. He didn't think he wanted to know. Then quietly in the dark, the horses took them deep into the trees, away from civilization. They were just clearing the ridge when the muffled sound of the gunshots rang out. With two quick pops, he knew they were gone. His anger reached a boiling point. His mind screamed, "You will pay for that, you bastard!" He knew he would make sure of that. As he turned away, he didn't hear the final shot. It was muffled and a smaller caliber weapon.

They rode late into the night and came to a cabin at the edge of the ridge just above the foothills. It was secluded, quiet, and well hidden. There they found the girl cooking on the old potbellied stove. She was startled at their arrival but quickly ran out and nearly pulled Tom from his horse as she jumped up and tried to hug him around the neck.

"Annie!" he gushed as he hugged her back.

They went inside, and she served them dinner. They ate quietly. As they ate, she relayed to them what she had seen and done up to when the old man had rescued her. She then sat and listened to Tom tell his story. Johnston asked the old man his name.

The old man just looked at him, shook his head

"I sometimes don't remember." He laughed. "I guess I am getting a little too old for this." He then walked over to a cot against the wall and lay down. In seconds he was snoring quietly.

Annie turned to Tom and whispered:

"Remember the 'Ancient Mysteries' episode I was watching when you snuck out?" He nodded, and she continued. "He is the Chosen…"

Tom looked back at the old man sleeping there. He thought of Sarah and the old Fortune Teller. What was that old lady saying as he left, some prayer for the Chosen? It couldn't be, yet there he was.

Johnston was struggling with what he should do. He knew he should go to the next safe house. He had to protect them, but he also knew that he could never trust the safe house. He decided that this cabin was most likely the safest place to be right now. No one would know where they were now. He could not call in his report. It would give them away. He stopped Tom at the door. "Wait up there, Tom. Where do you think you're going?" he asked.

"I have to find Sarah; she is in danger now too," said Tom. His voice was shaking.

"You can't help her now. You stay and protect Annie." He thought for a moment. "If you go riding into town, they will notice you for sure. Give me a minute or two… I will have to think of a way to ensure she is safe."

The sound at the door startled them. They turned together, both pointing their guns at the old Cherokee standing there.

"He was invited. Put your guns down," said the old man as he was sitting up on the cot. "Chief, come on in, and thanks for coming down."

The old Cherokee hesitated and just looked at the two until they lowered their guns. He then apologized for startling them. He came inside and sat with the old man at the table.

"Chosen, what do you require?" he asked.

The old man and the Chief looked at each other for a moment. Both had the same deep hardness in their eyes. They seemed to have a conversation without speaking. The old man then asked Tom to tell the Chief about Sarah and where he last saw her.

Tom told of the fortune teller and the stall where she promised to hide Sarah. The Chief nodded.

"I know the old woman well. If she is keeping Sarah safe, she will need help soon. Her magic is not as strong as it used to be. I will go now and offer my assistance. If I find them well they will stay that way. If not," he turned to the old man, "I welcome the chance to ride with you as my Grandfather did."

"Thankee," said the old man, "I welcome you to join me."

The Cherokee left, walked out of the clearing, and disappeared into the trees. He seemed to fade into the shadows long before he should have been out of sight.

The old man turned to Tom and Agent Johnston and said, "Sit down, gentlemen; I need to learn more about who is against us." He turned to Agent Johnston… "First, what is your name?"

"Francis Johnston," he answered with no hesitation. He was compelled to respond—he could lie to this man. He was uncomfortable in his stare, caught.

"Will Frank do?" asked the old man.

"Sure."

The old man turned to Thomas, "Annie said your name is Thomas. Would you prefer Tom?"

Tom nodded.

"Good, now tell me, just who am I up against?"

"What is your name, sir?" asked Tom.

The old man looked at him. "I am—" he paused, his brow furrowed. "My name is Teach, Caleb Teach."

The look of pain that crossed his face was startling. It was as if he was reliving an excruciating memory—a memory that passed as quickly as it came.

"Yes," he spoke almost to himself, "my name is Caleb Teach." He then looked up at them and continued, "It has been a long time since I spoke my own name. It seems it is time to hear it again."

He smiled, and as he did, it seemed that his face was creased with scars: scars of old physical and mental battles. Despite this, his eyes seemed to soften. Then he was back to the business at hand, and they answered all his questions. They spoke for a long time, each telling what they knew, believed, or just suspected. Even Annie interjected thoughts of her own. Tom was surprised at how much she had come to know. She had paid more attention than he had at her age. Caleb finally stopped them and told them to all get some rest. He would wake them when he heard back from the Chief.

They went in to find that there was a bed for each of them. They all lay down and were asleep faster than they ever expected possible.

Caleb watched them. After they were asleep, he walked out to the front of the cabin and closed the door. He sat on the stump of an old oak tree that had been chopped down nearly 80 years ago and pondered his new situation.

'I am Caleb and the Chief is here—or his grandson, rather. He looks the same, though. What does it mean?'

He thought over everything he had heard the others talking about. He didn't understand the parts about computers. He had no idea what they were. He didn't really care much beyond figuring out that they provided information he used to have to question many people to find out.

He still couldn't believe the year was 2005. That was something he was amazed by. Many people in his time thought the world would end long before the end of the 1800s. The way the world was going back then, he had suspected it to be true. He waited for nearly half the night before the Chief showed up again. He had the girl with him but not the old woman. Caleb looked in his eyes; the Chief just shook his head and looked upward for just a moment. Caleb knew she was gone. The girl looked frightened, but she was holding her own. Caleb signaled to the Chief to take her to the cabin. "Put her to bed, we will have much to discuss in the morning."

6

The Mercenary

The office was chilled to nearly 50 degrees. The others in the office were uncomfortable, but he didn't care. That was how he liked it so the rest could go hang. He slammed his fist against the desk, knocking over the pencil holder.

"What do you mean, they got away?" he glared at the Mercenary sitting across from him. "Did I make a mistake protecting your men at the trial? And don't tell me it wasn't your fault. You assured me that you would have them all in one night. So, anyone that was missed, I consider to be your fault."

"I would never consider shifting the blame, sir." said the Merc, "I chose the team leader; I chose the team. If they fucked it up, it is my fault, and if allowed, I will proceed to correct this issue."

Again the man's fist struck the desk. "That is the only answer I would accept and the only reason you are still alive." The man's face was flushed with anger, but his eyes betrayed nothing but cool, calculating business. "What is the status of Johnston and his team?"

"Johnston's team is dead," said the Merc, "including your inside man; we can't afford that loose end. As for Johnston, he got away. He had help; three of my men were taken out at the safe house. It seemed like they were hit with arrows, but there were no arrows left behind. So whoever did it came back and took them. No cars were seen leaving. The computer was wiped, so we won't know what they were doing from that."

The man interrupted him, "And the package they were holding?"

"He is gone with Johnston," the Merc said, "to wherever they've gone." He met the gaze coming back across the desk at him. "My team will find them. You will not be implicated."

"I have your word on that," said the man, "I will hold you to it. Now get out and don't be seen."

"No one saw me come in, and no one will ever see me here," said the Merc, as he got up and left quickly.

He had been thinking hard, trying to figure out what went wrong. They had everyone in place. The boy was supposed to be there, but he was not. He had dispatched men to the mall to get him when they overheard the conversation with the girl and her mother. The girl getting away was a slip-up, but that should have been handled already. Why Mac was not back yet concerned him, but that was not new for Mac. That crazy bastard would be enjoying himself for a while, but the Merc couldn't imagine the girl might get away from him.

His team at the mall had not reported in yet. They should be back within the hour. The girl Sarah was to be brought in. She would have to be kept alive to keep the boy in line, and his orders were that she was not to be harmed in any way. The boy was key: the only one in the family other than the father who knew where the evidence was hidden. The Merc needed to get that evidence.

To ensure he was protected, the boy's father was giving the evidence out one little bit at a time. He would provide the information they asked about an individual of interest but never offered to give all he knew at one time. He thought he was protecting his family that way. It turned out he was wrong. Other people could pay more for that information or to keep that information hidden. He'd paid for that mistake with his wife's life, his own, and nearly the lives of his entire family. The Merc promised himself he was going to find them. He had to.

7

Caleb and the Chief

Caleb and the Chief had been speaking for several hours. The Chief knew more of modern times. His life followed a different path than the Chosen. He was not always called to the task, but on rare occasions, the Chief was needed. He would always be there when called—not the same man in body but always the same man in spirit and conviction. This time, the Chief looked older, more tired but just as wise, and it was he who had to provide the Chosen with the needed details of the present times.

Had the Chief not shown up at the cabin before Caleb went to find Tom, he would have been unprepared for the cars and other motor vehicles tearing up the roads. The Chief also brought him the horses, saying he would need them. Somehow the Chief had known. As they spoke, a helicopter a few miles to the south turned away. They had been scanning the area, searching. They saw the cabin, but the horses, Caleb, and the Chief were not who they were looking for. The Chief looked after the chopper as it sped off.

"You will have to watch out for those; they can see you sitting here as plain as if they were standing here with us if they try. It is good that everyone was inside before that thing was near. Listen for that sound and be prepared to take cover."

"So many things are strange now," said Caleb. "Flying coaches and I have seen horseless carriage before, but they never went faster than a horse at a trot. These are so fast; how do they control them?"

The Chief thought a moment.

"Yes, they have created many wonderful things. But like most things man builds, they have used these wonders to devastating effects." The Chief looked Caleb deeply in the eyes. "Chosen, this will be our last time working together. Always a son is born to take the knowledge, but my son was killed in the wars of this time before I could teach him our ways. My Grandson is also gone, lost to these times as well. My Great Grandson is not of an age where I can begin to teach or pass along the duties." Caleb saw a deep sadness and regret in the old Chief's eyes.

"It has been my honor to be kin to you and your family," he told the Chief.

They sat silently for a while, knowing all and yet not knowing what path the future would hold for them both. After a silent moment, they began planning the next move.

8

Gray

The Horse was watching the old men. He could tell they were worried by the loud machine in the sky. He had seen them before; they would chase the horses. He was always able to escape, but they would capture some of his herd. He hated them, and he was nervous now.

Suddenly, the girl's voice was there at his side:

"Hello, Gray." She said. "Sarah is finally sleeping, so I came out to take care of you." He recognized the name she had given him. He nickered and pounded his hoof in the ground. She patted his nose, and he pulled his attention away from the men and turned to look at her.

The girl was gentle and stroked his nose and presented him an apple. He liked her—she was different from the other people he had met. He trusted her more than anyone besides the old man. She soothed him with her voice as she brushed him. She cared for all the horses but spent extra time with Gray. Because of this, he was calmer with her.

He had watched the old man show her how to rub them down after a ride, brush them, and feed them. She would make sure all the horses were ready when needed. Gray was still wild, in a way, but he would never fight when she came with the bridle and saddle. When the old man was not using him, Gray would let her climb on his back. She would brush his mane and walk him around the small corral. No person other than the old man would dare come alone to stand close to him; he wouldn't let them. But the girl, she was different. He would protect her, as he had seen the old man defend her.

When she had finished with Gray, she moved to the other two horses and brushed them as well. He turned his head and tried to nuzzle her as she left; she patted his nose again.

"Don't worry; I will come back to you." She giggled a little when he pushed her with his nose, but she finished her duty by the other horses. She then fed them hay gathered from the stack by the house. She gave them each an apple and grain from the bag giving him more than the others.

"Gray, I am counting on you. Protect Caleb and Tom when you go out again." She patted his nose and spoke very earnestly. She hugged his head and gave him the last piece of her apple. "Sorry, it's not the ones you like best. Hornets have moved into that tree; I can't get to the green ones." She gave his nose one more stroke then walked back to the cabin. He watched her walk away. He didn't understand why he was drawn to her. With the old man, he felt he had no choice. He was frightened by the old man; he always smelled remotely of death. The old man had cared for him well and had even taught the girl.

He had felt genuine affection from the girl. He still didn't trust men, but she could come to him without any worry. After she entered the cabin, he turned to look back where the men had been talking. The old chief was gone without a trace. The old man was looking at him as he stood facing the corral. He felt the same chill he always felt.

The old man smiled, then walked over and stroked his nose. "You have a new friend?" he asked. He pulled a carrot out of his pocket. Fed it to him, "Gray huh?" the old man seemed to roll the name around in his mind then spoke again: "Yes, that is a good name for you, much better than just calling you Horse. I expect you will take care of her when you have to. I can't say why, Gray, but this time feels so different. I have been thinking I will not see you again after this adventure." Gray didn't understand the words, but he felt the sense of the old man's words besides. He still felt fear around the old man, but he respected him. The old man was dangerous, but not to Gray. He would protect them. They were now his herd.

9

Jamison

"The whole team?" the Section Chief Ward Jamison asked, "and Johnston and his charge are missing?"

"Yes." It was the only answer they had for now. "We are still investigating. It seems like they were following protocol when they were ambushed. Someone knew they were there. There was blood and evidence of several people being killed around the property. However, only three bodies were found. Two were shot execution-style on the porch. The third looks as if he was watching the execution. Then he was shot from behind as well."

"He must have been the mole," said the Admin.

"That is what we suspect," said the man giving the briefing. "It appears they took the bodies of their own men and just left our men behind where they fell. We suspect that our third man had turned weeks ago and was waiting for an opportunity. In hindsight, we have found some evidence indicating payments to him and minor attempts to access data beyond his pay scale."

"And why wasn't this flagged?"

"All was shown to be part of an ongoing investigation; the

requests were just far enough within parameters to escape notice."

The Section Chief just looked at them all. His gaze passed from one to the next ensuring they all knew he was deadly serious. "We will have to revisit these parameters in the very near future," he stated simply. The implications were evident in his tone.

"Yes, Sir," they said in unison.

"For now, do we have any information about the girlfriend, Sarah," he paused a moment struggling to remember her full name.

"Abraham, Sir," said the other man. "She was last seen leaving the Mall with an older woman and an older man. Witnesses said it looked as if they were trying to protect her. However, the older woman was found later, two blocks away. She appeared to have been struck in the head." He paused. "Someone was chasing them. We don't know if Miss Abraham escaped with the old man or not."

Jamison just sat there. It was going to be a difficult call to tell her parents that their daughter was missing. He would have to find out about the family before the call. He hated making these calls cold. He had to work fast, though; this was going to be challenging to keep out of the press for long, and he knew he had to call them before they found out on some news program.

"Okay, Agents," he said, "Get out there, find our charges, and find them alive. If we lose people we have under protection, we may have trouble getting witnesses in the future."

The agents dispersed, going back to their investigations. Jamison sat for a moment before making the next call to his director Jim Forrester.

"Sir?" he said. After listening for a moment or two, he looked down at his desk. The look on his face was hard to read.

"No, Sir," he said, "but I am going to find out, and we will have this cleaned up as soon as possible."

Ward listened a moment, and his face darkened with anger. "No, Sir," he said, "Johnston is not a turncoat. If anything, I would say he would be the best one you could hang your trust on in times like this. He will not fail his charges. If anyone can protect them in this, it is him."

"Are you sure you can trust him?" asked the voice on the other end of the line.

Jamison spoke in the affirmative—with less conviction this time.

"Very well. Get to work then and find these VIPs. And don't let me down," the voice responded.

10

Sarah

Annie knew that they were alone when she woke up. The cabin was too quiet. There was something that smelled very good. The aroma made her want to see what it was, but she didn't get up yet. It was late in the morning and later than she usually had slept since coming to the cabin. When the Chief had brought Sarah, Annie had stayed up with her to help her to adjust to the stress and shock. Sarah had told her how they had tried to slip away, but they had been spotted before they had gone two blocks. They had been chased and cornered in the abandoned mansion's backyard. The two men thought they would be able to take Sarah easily, but the Chief proved to be much more skilled than they had ever expected. The old chief fought to protect them. One man broke past and came after Sarah. He raised his club intending to knock her out, but the old woman had jumped in front of her when the man was swinging the club. The Chief had just knocked the other man out and couldn't get back to Sarah before this man swung his club.

The old woman had sacrificed herself to protect Sarah. The

chief reached them before the man could grab Sarah and quickly disarmed and used the man's own club to dispatch him. They didn't wait to see if he was still alive. The Chief checked the old woman, looked up at Sarah, and just shook his head, then took her arm and led her away. They could do nothing for her, which was the most difficult thing for Sarah to handle.

She had cried late into the night, and Annie had held her till she fell asleep. After slipping out to take care of the horses, Annie had slept on the bed next to Sarah's. She looked across at the other bed. Sarah was still asleep, but she was not sleeping soundly. There were still tears on her face. Annie knew she was dreaming of it all over again. She sat up and reached over to take Sarah's hand. Just the touch seemed to ease Sarah's nightmare. She waited for Sarah's breathing to settle down.

Annie got up and pulled on her jeans. She went to the kitchen following the scent of the food. As she had thought, no one was there. The girls were alone in the cabin. She was a little nervous, but she had stayed here by herself a few times while Caleb was away. The kitchen was neat and tidy. The Chief had cleaned up the men's breakfast and had put away the dishes. There were two plates on the table, and next to them, propped against the cup, was a note.

Miss Annie,

I have left your breakfast in the oven. It should be ready for you. Please make sure Sarah eats, it will help her settle in. Caleb has taken Agent Johnston and Tom to retrieve documents to turn them in.

Caleb will keep them safe. I may return sooner than they will.

Take care of Sarah and the horses. Stay alert. Hide if you hear or see anyone.

I go to honor Lady Maribel.

Annie heard Sarah getting up. She checked the oven. The pot was bubbling and looked and smelled wonderful. The Chief's breakfast was going to be just what they needed. Annie served up two plates and set them on the table as Sarah came out of the room. Annie motioned for her to sit and join her. At first, she didn't think she could eat, but as she sat there with Annie, the aroma of the food sparked her hunger, and she took a bite. The food turned out to be wonderful and helped her feel closer to normal. It was filling and warmed her from the inside out. Annie showed her the note. They didn't speak for several minutes as they ate until Sarah looked up from her plate, "Horses?"

Annie smiled and said, "Yeah, they're beautiful. When we are done eating I'll introduce you. You can help me take care of them today."

Sarah looked out the back door. "I think I would like that. I've had riding lessons, but we never owned the horses and were never involved with taking care of them." Sarah thought that might be just the thing she needed. It would be good not to think of the lady.

"I didn't think Maribel was her real name," she said.

"I wish I had met her," Annie said.

They ate the rest of their meal, talking about the horses. Annie told Sarah how Caleb had taught her to care for the horses. She said she would show Sarah. For a few minutes, they could almost forget the events of the last couple of days, but it was always there. They both knew their lives would never be the same.

When they were done, they washed their dishes together. They put away the leftovers and got ready to go outside. Annie took Sarah out the back door. It was hidden from the side of the mountain. No one would see them as they walked between the trees over to the corral.

They each had two handfuls of hay, and Annie carried the grain bag over her shoulder. She passed a small sack to Sarah and asked her to grab some apples from the trees by the cabin.

"Gray likes the green ones, but that tree has a hornet nest, so I haven't been able to get them."

Sarah looked at the nest and said, "I can get them; bees and wasps don't ever sting me; I don't see why hornets would be different." She walked up to the tree, picked several, and quickly placed them in the sack. Annie watched her as hornets flew around her. Some landed on her but flew away. Sarah then walked over to the other tree and picked several red apples. The hornets circled her till she turned and walked away from the trees.

Annie watched her as the hornets returned to their nest. Sarah smiled at the surprised look on Annie's face. "That was amazing," said Annie. "How do you do that?"

Sarah just shrugged, "I don't know; they just never sting me."

The girls continued on their way to the corral. They worked quietly. Annie showed Sarah how to use the curry comb on the horses. She introduced Sarah to the horses one at a time until they came over to Gray. Sarah could see the affection between the two. This horse seemed to nod to her when Annie introduced her. She reached out and patted his nose. He twitched his ears, nuzzled Annie, and turned his face towards Sarah. He wiggled his ears at her, then took the green apple Sarah offered. The girls giggled and laughed as Gray gently leaned against Annie.

11

Honoring Miss Maribel

The Chief walked into the morgue. No one seemed to notice him dressed in scrubs that were just a bit too small. The name badge that he wore made it appear as though he were a new employee with a name written in black marker. The ink had smudged as if it had brushed against something—just enough to make the characters too difficult to make out. He didn't draw attention as he pushed the gurney through the hall.

When he got to the double door, he just pushed through as if he had an assigned task. Most of the others didn't look at him, as they suspected the job to which he was assigned in the morgue was one they were glad had not been assigned to them.

He found himself alone in the room with her. He quickly found her possessions in the Ziploc bags labeled and prepped for next of kin. At that time around shift change, there would be few people near this room, so he would have time to do what was needed.

The Chief leaned over her and presented her with a low chant. His deep voice, resonating but quiet, seemed to brighten the room around her. He opened the bag, pulled her necklace out, and removed the charm from the center. He held the charm out above her and felt her essence pass through the pendant into his chant. Her spirit was released to the next world through his words and song. She was no longer captive and would become a spirit guide for the next Oracle to be born into the world.

He had honored her as was his duty and now finished his task. He returned the necklace to the bag, but he held the charm—that talisman he must pass on. It was his duty to find the next to ensure they received the gift. He hoped he would live long enough to pass it on. He would have to find a way.

When the echoes of his song faded, he placed the bag exactly where it had been. With luck, no one would notice it had ever been tampered with. He left the gurney and walked out a different door than through which he had entered. He slipped into a side room and changed back into his clothes. As he left the room, he walked across the hall and left the envelope on the counter. It was addressed simply with a note indicating a final burial request for the old woman. Inside was the contact information for the funeral parlor. All arrangements had been made for her. He walked out the back hallway to the parking lot exit without pausing.

12

The Chief

The man watched as the Chief moved from the building. To the man, it looked as though the Chief thought no one had seen him leave. But the man did see, and now he stealthily followed. The soldier watched the Chief move through the parking lot into the shadows behind the building and then into the alley. The man was ducking between cars so he wouldn't be seen. The chief was gone when he turned to follow his target down the alley. There was no way the Chief could have gone the entire length of the alley in that time. The man checked all the shadows as he walked, looking left and right not seeing any sign of the Chief. At the end of the alley, he looked both ways down the street, but there was no one there. The man shuddered. He felt fear for the first time since he was a child.

Maybe this is a job I shouldn't have accepted, he thought.

He turned to run back down the alley to go to his car, and in two strides, he was face-to-face with the Chief, who hadn't been there moments ago; before the soldier could react, the Chief's hard fist met his chin, and he was relieved of any further thoughts for the next several hours.

13

Tom Returns Home

Caleb watched as Tom and Frank steadily crept to the back gate. He had their escape route covered in case someone spotted them. He had wanted the boy to stay behind, but he had to come along. He could disarm the alarms before they went off. They needed him to go, or their job would be too difficult. Tom could do the task and get out more quickly than either of them could have done it.

Tom looked through the hole in the fence. The space beyond was clear. He shot a look at Frank and motioned him to the spot. Frank looked as well and confirmed that he too saw nothing. But he was still hesitant. There was a portion of the yard they could not see from that vantage point.

They looked back at the tree line they had just left. At first, Tom could not see Caleb, then noticed a slight movement from among the trees. It was Caleb indicating for them to sit still. They remained motionless, almost holding their breath. Slowly Frank turned his head back and looked through the hole and then saw the man walking away from the corner of the yard. He had been searching the backyard. He had not seen anything and was leaving. There were windows on this side of the house, but no one could see this corner of the yard without opening them and leaning out. His father put in the gate to allow an unseen exit from the shed to the woods behind the house. That had saved his sister, and now it was his way to get back in.

They looked back at Caleb. He gave the all-clear. Tom opened the gate, and they entered the yard quietly.

Tom slid on his belly behind the shed to the back of the brick chimney of the outdoor kitchen. Frank followed close behind. Tom rose to his knees and slowly pulled a brick out; then the second brick, carefully handing them to Frank so as not to break off the grout that kept the opening hidden. Frank placed the bricks on the ground with care. Tom kept removing one brick after the other until he revealed a small door behind the bricks. Tom entered the combination and slowly opened the door. Hidden inside the insulated box was a second keypad—anyone who missed that one would trip the alarms. Tom entered the second code by touch.

Tom lifted from the ground just enough to look into the opening while remaining hidden behind the BBQ pit. There he saw several jump drives and documents. He took the jump drives, placed several of them in his pockets, and handed more to Frank. When they had them all, he flipped a lever inside the box. It opened the insulation on the inside of the box and slid the side down.

He closed the outer door and carefully replaced the bricks in proper order as Frank handed them back to him. The opening was invisible when he finished, as though no one had been there.

When they had finished, Tom and Frank slid back behind

the shed. They looked back up at Caleb. He had his bow ready; they could see his hand poking from the trees beside a readied arrow. They both stiffened, wondering if they had been seen.

Their worry proved unfounded as Caleb lowered the point a few inches and motioned them to the gate. They slid through and closed it behind them silently.

They were about to move when they heard someone open the grill cover behind them. They listened to the firelight, and Tom smiled. The documents would char and burn away in minutes with the chimney box opened. No one would notice the records going up with the smoke of the grill. Tom looked through the hole to see smoke rising. They were away free and clear. When the meat started to sizzle, they crept back along the fence to the trees. Caleb led them back up the trail and away.

"We will need a laptop with airgap security to open these files. We can't disable the security built into their software; it will notify the server with our GPS locations. So no Wi-Fi, network, or Bluetooth at all," Tom said.

Frank looked at him. "I can get to one of those."

As Frank was speaking, Tom looked at Caleb. It was clear that he didn't understand what they were speaking of,

"A computer is a tool; we use it to get information and send these documents to Frank's boss.

"Like the telegraph?" he asked.

"Essentially, yes," said Tom, and more."

Caleb nodded; Tom didn't bother trying to explain in detail. Once he knew Caleb saw this as a tool, he decided to wait till he had it in hand; he would show Caleb then. It would be easier to explain.

14

The Mercenary

The girls had stayed in the shadows of the trees going to the back of the corral so that

no one could see them. But while they were in the corral, someone did see them. He had watched them through binoculars for a few minutes. He decided that neither of these girls was the one he was searching for. They couldn't be. The Merc lowered his binoculars, got back on his motorcycle, and rode on. The girls were lucky—the food and the horses had lifted their spirits just enough that the man looking for Sarah couldn't believe they could be that happy so soon after the woman had died. It didn't occur to him that the other girl could be the daughter.

His missing man had called and said he had her. Knowing Mac, he figured the pervert was toying around and enjoying her too long. He had to get that prick again and put him back on the job. Mac was getting worse; the Merc may have to end their association. For now, though, the Merc would keep searching. He had no other choice. He would keep this cabin in his mind to check again later. For now, he had to find his missing man. The girls never knew how close they had come to being discovered.

The Mercenary continued his search on the motorcycle. He was halfway down the mountain heading back on the narrow roadway towards the house when he saw something out of place. He turned around and headed back up the street. Beside the road was a horse trail leading off at an angle from where he was riding; he could see fabric flapping in the breeze.

He stopped the bike, dropped the kickstand, and killed the engine. He climbed down the ditch and up the other side. There he picked up a piece of fabric. Immediately he recognized it as a bit of torn cloth from a shirt pocket. He looked around the tree, stepped over the roots, and walked into a small clearing. There he saw the drag marks. He followed them up the hillside until they dropped into a small depression.

That was where he found Mac, or rather what was left of him. There was a jagged bloody hole in the back of his shirt. The Mercenary knelt to examine closer. The wound in the man's body was narrow but deep. Whatever hit him had severed his spine. He would have died quickly, but it would have hurt like hell while it happened.

The Mercenary suspected the wound was from an arrow. He could also tell that it had caused considerably more damage on the way out than it had on the way in as if the one pulling it out didn't care about causing more pain. The Mercenary began to wonder just what he and his team were involved in now.

He had worked for this client in the past and had never had any complaints. However, he had lost several men in short order on this job. Now one more here, and he had yet to hear a report back from the man at the hospital. His mind was racing.

Two men were sent to capture a young couple at the mall. That should have been easy, but they had managed to mess up that operation. They had figured out that they lost the boy at the old lady's fortune teller tent. He must have left the girl there, but the men had not found her. Then of the eight men he sent to the safe house to grab the kid again, he had lost another three. He had sent two men back to the mall after the girl and the old woman. They killed the woman, but yet another one of them had died. The Mercenary had sent the other back to the hospital to watch for someone to check on the old woman's body. They needed some kind of lead. However, that man was no longer responding to communications.

His anger rose. This was the worst performance he had ever received from his team. He had to find his remaining mercs and get this job back on track. He walked back to the bike. As he was fastening his helmet, an old man stepped out onto the road from the path. There was a bow in his hand. The Merc pushed his dirt bike forward without starting it so it would roll silently before revving to life.

The old man turned to him, and his eyes turned the Merc's blood to ice. Just cold gray malice shining there. He didn't wait; he just pushed the starter and rode past the stranger as fast as he could.

He felt the arrow fly past as the old man let loose. He pushed his bike faster than the curved road should have allowed. He was unsure how he kept from going over the edge, but he stayed upright.

There was no way he was going to go against those eyes without his team. He rode for half a mile before stopping. He suddenly remembered his gun, unsure how he had been so frozen by fear that he forgot it. Those eyes, the memory of them, kept him shaking. After a minute, he calmed himself. Anger replaced his fear. He had never been that filled with anxiety before, and he would not let someone live who could do that to him.

He told himself it was just being surprised by the older man's appearance so soon after finding Mac dead. He should not have been filled with fear like that. He would never let it happen again.

15

Caleb

Caleb walked across the paved road and checked for his arrow. He found it buried in a small tree. The arrow had gone through the tree, and the head protruded an inch through the other side. He could not pull it out. He pulled his knife and cut the shaft to recover the arrowhead and again to recover the feathers from the other end. He would have to make a new arrow with them. He heard the motorcycle down the roadway.

That was a strange beast. He thought as he strode back to the roadway.

He whistled the signal to Tom and Frank. They stepped from behind the trees and followed him as he led them up the path to the drag marks. He led them to the body.

"Don't step near those tracks," said Caleb, "we need them to remain where they are." He turned to Frank and pointed to the body. "You know him?"

Frank knelt and looked at the face. He nodded.

"Yeah, this guy is on our watch list for his military crimes and was wanted for questioning in several assault cases involving young women."

Frank then turned to Tom. "Last I heard, he was in Africa, and we couldn't get to him. He sells his services to several mercenary groups. We are in trouble if that's who we are against here."

"I guess you can stop looking for him now." Tom stared at the man.

"We need to keep going," said Caleb, "that other'n stopped down the road. He is going to come back. I have seen it before. He can't stand that something scared him."

"What should we do about him," Frank said.

"Not sure; I didn't mean to miss him." Caleb thought for a moment. "He probably won't come back alone. His kind never does. We better cover our tracks. You guys go through the trees up to the ridge. I will meet you there."

Frank and Tom started to protest, but Caleb's eyes showed he would not accept any other choices.

"Step on thick roots and rocks on the way up as much as possible. I will clear your tracks from here. No one but the Chief will be able to tell you were here," was all he said.

Tom and Frank continued up through the trees towards the ridge. Caleb went down to the edge of the roadway. He looked both ways and made sure there were no sounds. He cleared the tracks and then left just his own behind. The man had seen him and would be expecting to see his tracks. He walked back to where the body was lying. He checked his bearings and then went a different direction from the body for a short distance to a creek bed and started down the stream walking in the water as if he was trying to hide his tracks. When he got to the rocks, he stepped up and left one muddy footprint pointing west in the direction of the stream. He grabbed the branch above the rock and hung for a minute while the stream cleared the mud from his boots. Then he pulled himself up out of the water. He was careful not to bend or break any small branches as he brought himself hand over hand to the other side of the stream. He dropped onto a rock on the other side of the tree and waited. When he was satisfied no one was following, he crept back further into the trees stepping on roots and rocks, leaving no footprints.

After several minutes he was back up on the ridge and striding towards Tom and Frank. They hiked back into the trees and around the long way back to the cabin along a well-worn path that would hide their tracks among the many others that were there.

At the cabin, Frank said that he needed to go report in. He was bothered that the Mercs were setting up in Tom's house. That place should still be under investigation as an active crime scene. These guys looked like they had moved in. He had to find out what was happening.

Caleb asked him to wait for the Chief to return, but Frank convinced him that the longer he was out of communication with his agency, the worse it could end up being for Tom and the kids. They worked it out that he would check for an empty safe house and set up there as if it was where they had been hiding. He could do it. Then he would present what he had found out so far. The mercenaries were something they had not expected. More importantly, he had to report the fact that someone on the inside had breached the security. This was something he had to report sooner than later. He did not know how far up it went, but he would shake the tree from his office and see what would fall.

He checked the girls and was satisfied they were OK. After

they spoke to the girls about the Mercenary on the motorcycle, Sarah shuddered.

"I heard a motorcycle earlier." She said.

"When?" Annie asked.

"While Gray was making us laugh, I didn't think anything of it," she said. "Motorcycles ride these trails all the time."

The Chief was walking in the door as she said this. "We need to move then," he said.

Caleb nodded. "You know where to take them, Chief. Best get going."

"Girls, get the horses ready." Annie and Sarah jumped to the task.

"Chief," said Caleb, "you take Tom and the girls where they will be safe." Tom started to protest, but Caleb shook his head.

"Get along quickly, and don't worry about buttoning this place down," he said. "Leave the cabin as it is. I will take Frank with me and get him to his safe house."

He turned away before Tom could say anything.

"Where will they be?" asked Frank.

"Safe, that's all you need to know for now." Caleb turned away and led him out the door. He checked the saddles and smiled at the girls. He nodded, acknowledging their good work, slightly adjusted the tackle on Gray, and climbed up. He led the other two horses to the back door of the cabin.

The Chief took the reins as Tom helped Sarah up onto the horse. He climbed up behind her. She held the saddle horn, and Tom reached around and held the reins in front of her. Sarah giggled and took the reins from him. "Am I going to have to teach you to ride too?"

Tom held onto her waist and smiled. "Yeah, I think so," he said.

The Chief mounted with a chuckle, reached down, and pulled Annie up behind him in a gentle swing that settled her securely behind him. Then he swung the horse around and led them up the mountain trail as he quietly started chanting in his deep voice.

As Frank watched them go, it again seemed like they faded away long before they should have been out of sight.

Caleb looked down at him from the big horse. "Yeah, that always seemed strange to me too." Frank looked up at him with a confused look.

"That disappearing the Chief does," Caleb chuckled, "he never did teach me… could have been handy a time or two." Caleb's face clouded, and the look in his eyes was distant. As if he was not present in their time. After a minute, he shook his head as if to scatter bad memories away.

Caleb looked back at Frank, then reached down and grabbed his hand, and swung him up easily behind him on the horse. Frank was surprised at the strength of the old man.

"That's just part of his magic I guess." Caleb looked through the trees up the mountain trail. "No one can see him when he doesn't want to be seen. I didn't know he could hide others with him like that."

"It is a handy skill," said Frank

Caleb nodded and turned the horse down the other trail. They went through the trees down the trail from the mountain, then through the hills into the back end of a park.

They stopped there to observe the park. It was empty. There was no one there, but they still rode around the park in the tree line. Always watching across the park at the row of houses along the opposite side, they saw no one there. When they reached the paved path, Caleb turned them down the pavement. The paved path went along the backyards of the houses. They went across there till Frank signaled with a tap. Caleb left the path and approached the fence row behind a small nondescript home with a high fence. There Frank dismounted and reached for the gate. He paused before going through.

"How will I notify you of what I find?" he asked as he was watching the house. There was no answer. He turned, and Caleb and the horse were gone. There had been no sound of them leaving or moving through the trees. Frank shuddered.

"Like hell, he didn't teach you," he whispered to himself. Then he turned back to the task at hand.

He surveyed the house making sure it was vacant, then approached cautiously. He entered the house through the discrete doorway hidden from the street or any neighbors. Once inside he checked the house room by room. When satisfied that the house was clear, he went to the office. He opened the secure line and called Jamison directly.

16

Going Hunting

The Merc rode up to the back of Tom's house and parked his bike in the trees. He walked around the fence to the front gate in the yard. He slipped into the backyard and followed the aroma of the cooking meat. He found two of the men he had left here to watch the place sitting under the umbrella chowing on the freshly grilled steaks. He was still angry at himself for being frightened of the old man. In his mind, he was trying to convince himself that he had just been startled and was not scared.

He walked up to the men and spoke quietly:

"Why are you grilling instead of searching? You guys act like you never served in the military, but you have to be smart enough to know you were supposed to be watching for the kids to try to sneak back here instead of just enjoying yourselves."

They said, "We have watched for three days. Nobody has been here. Even the cops haven't been back."

"Well, someone was here. I ran into him up on the ridge behind the house. He was on the trail right up there." The Merc was pointing back up the mountain trails behind the house.

"Who? How would you know he came from here?"

"The arrow flying by my head as I went by him gave me a big clue." He glared at them. "You remember how our guys died when we tried to take the kid at the safe house?" he asked. When they nodded, he continued. "I found Mac out there. He was shot with an arrow like them. Who else do you think would be shooting arrows at me like that? Now get your asses in there, grab your gear, call our guys back in and get the rest of the team up on this damn mountain. I am even calling in Thompson and his team. We may need the extra men before this is over; we are going hunting for that old man." The Merc pulled out his secure satellite phone and called Thompson's contact. He hated the man but had to admit he was good for what he used him for. While he was waiting for the phone to connect, he looked at his men. "Well, get going!"

The phone call was quick; he provided the minimal instructions and locations for Thompson's contact to be ready.

The men left their steaks on the table and ran inside. As they were grabbing their bags, the Merc grabbed one of the steaks and took a bite.

Dumb shit can't even grill a good steak, he thought.

He took another bite and tossed it back on the table as the men came back out. He led them around to the back fence, then up the trail. When they got to Mac's body, he paused to let the men see how he died, then followed the path to the stream. He lost the tracks in the water for a bit as he expected the old man to go upstream. He turned back and found the disturbed rocks going downstream and followed. The path was hard to follow, but he had tracked men through streams before and was confident he was on the right trail now. Then he found the muddy print on the rock. This confirmed he was going the right way. He headed downstream a little faster as his anger drove him for several yards.

His thoughts were disturbed, and he realized the trail had ended. He was not thinking. He stopped and stood up. He was better than this; he knew it. He couldn't figure out what was going wrong. He turned and went back to the rock. The footprint disturbed him. It just didn't seem right. Someone so good at hiding his path wouldn't have left a muddy print on the rock. He stood there with his men looking at him.

Which way? He thought. He looked around then up and saw the branches. It would be quite a leap, but a tall man could reach them. He made his decision and turned to his men.

"Go check around the trees over there," he pointed to the far side of the stream, "I'll check this side. Look for any signs of someone going through the trees."

He turned and stepped into the trees slowly. He was aware of every sound now. His anger had left, and he was calm and thinking again now. He searched again and started thinking about how he would get out of here without tracks. Then he figured it had to be the roots and rocks. Someone could carefully walk through here and never touch the mud. He started looking for minor marks on the bark of the roots. It took longer than it should, but when he was sure there was nothing on this side, he went back across the stream to where his men searched for signs. There he saw the scratch on the roots bark. He couldn't be sure it wasn't one of his men who left the mark, so he followed a bit further and found another. Then he saw a rock that looked to have been recently pushed down by a weight. He motioned his men to follow quietly, and they followed the trail back up the hill. Halfway up, he found where the old man had stopped trying to hide his path. It was clear he was going straight up the mountain. They followed up to the ridge and the path. The old man's tracks moved uphill and merged with the hikers and horses who used this trail. He had a sinking feeling as they followed the path. It led past a clearing, and at the other end was the cabin he had observed from the motorcycle trail earlier today. His anger flared up again, but he kept control this time.

Let it burn, he thought. *Use it.*

His anger at the old man grew as he realized this man had saved the girl. Those two he saw earlier were the girls he was searching for. He cursed himself silently as he thought of his mistake. He radioed his other teams, gave them the coordinates of the cabin, and told them to meet him there.

He led the men with him cautiously through the trees to take up a position to keep watch. When the rest of his men arrived, he had nearly three squads. They executed a very professional approach to the house. They kept to shadows and moved only when they were sure they weren't seen. They aligned themselves and entered the front and back at the same time with weapons drawn.

No one was there. Everything was cleaned, but all equipment was out. The place looked like it was prepped for a long season. Like everyone should be sitting around enjoying themselves—just no people. He cursed himself again and told his men to search for tracks leading away. They found horse tracks, two sets leading into the woods on the uphill side, going down towards the park. The horses going uphill disappeared onto the trail mixed with the hiker, biker, and horse prints from the people that used the path up there. They could not follow them.

The tracks leading down, however, did not follow a standard trail. These they could observe easily. Their decision was made for them; they followed.

17

The Chief

The Chief had led them carefully to the main trail. He knew horses, hikers, and even the occasional ATV often used this trail. He suspected that their tracks would be hidden soon within the traces left by others. They passed several other horses led by riders on trail tours of the mountain. There was another following them.

They also passed a few hikers. The Chief was relieved that the trail would be covered so quickly. He led them further into the mountain to a rocky and quick stream. He led the horses up the creek for about a half-hour, then arrived at a smaller cabin. This one looked very old and had runes carved on the posts on either side of the porch. Vines were growing up into the logs of the walls, and the roof looked to have been grown from the grass. A small opening beside the cabin led to a fenced-in hidden corral for the horses. A small shed was there to provide them shelter from the sun or rain when it came. He helped Annie down and dismounted. He did not let them walk straight up to the cabin. Instead, he handed Annie the reins and told Tom to get down. He held the reins as Tom helped Sarah down. They then led the horses through the trees around the clearing to the back of the corral. They removed the saddles and placed them in the shed, and the blankets were laid over the beam. They first cared for the horses. Annie and Sarah grained them as the Chief checked their hooves and legs for injury. Satisfied the horses were well, they left the horses to graze and closed up the corral. He led the small group through the trees to the back of the cabin, surveyed the clearing with his eyes, and listened to the animals and wind in the trees. All these sounds told him the cabin was undisturbed. He still cautiously stepped to the back door by himself and went in to verify. Moments later, he was back at the door and signaled them to come quietly.

They were all inside the cabin with the door shut. If not for the two horses, the place still looked abandoned, and the corral could not be seen except straight above due to the trees. This was the Chief's own family home. He was born here and knew this side of the mountain. These animals knew him. They would be his early warning. If anyone approached, he would know. In his thoughts, he lamented not having an heir to whom he could pass these teachings on. He knew his great-grandson would never reach the age of learning before the Chief was gone. Even if he was of that age now, there was no way to make the boy understand the need to learn everything the Chief needed to teach.

Annie asked him why he looked so sad. The Chief smiled at her.

"Do not let my inner pain be a worry for you, young lady. I was only thinking of my son, who I lost."

"I am so sorry," Annie said. She reached out to him and touched his arm.

He was surprised, not by the touch nor by her sentiment but rather by the sensation of the hair on his arms standing up. She had the spirit in her. He had never felt this himself, but his Grandfather had said about him when his teaching had begun.

He looked into her eyes. She looked back, and he was staring at the deepest soul he had ever seen in a child of her age. She did not turn away from his gaze as most people would. Yes, she had the spirit. It called to him.

"Annie, you are a child of the Spirit," he said without realizing it until after he said it. Annie looked at him and frowned a little.

"You must learn," he said. "I must teach. Will you accept my instruction?"

"Yes," she answered. They then broke eye contact.

Tom and Sarah were speaking. They had not seemed to notice the conversation between Annie and the Chief.

18

The Hunt

Frank hung up the phone. Ward Jamison had listened and then confirmed the same calls that Frank had seen. He had verified the security tapes for the phone banks. The agent they suspected had given up the safe house was there making the calls that gave up the family's location. Frank told him the kids were safe. He spoke of the mercenaries at the family's house. Jamison said he would send a team over. He would also check why the police were not watching the place. Frank hung up and cleared the line. He then opened the laptop that was there. He turned off all network cards and disabled all wireless connections. He made sure the computer was not connected to any network. He pulled the jump drives out of his bag and locked them in the safe in the floor under the table. When the door to the safe closed, there remained no indication that anything had ever been there. He kept one jump drive and put it in the USB port. He started reading.

The documents there were unbelievable. There were accounts, registers, and hierarchy.

The names were false, but the amounts of deposits and

withdrawals were staggering. Several of these false names had been revealed piecemeal by Tom's father. Frank began studying the documents. He needed to figure out who these names represented. He pulled out his notepad and pen. He began to jot down his thoughts and plans to research. One way or the other he would expose these people and protect the kids. This had become his sole purpose for the time being.

Even as he was intently focused on his task and the documents, the Mercenary was across the park. The trail he had been following led to a paved path. It went straight through the park, but there was a fork halfway. He had to be careful to pick the right way. He and his men were staying in the trees remaining out of sight. He felt as if someone was watching. After several minutes, he noticed a strange lack of noise from the trees. No birds. No animal noises at all. This disturbed him, so he kept still. After several minutes he dismissed his feeling of unease and waved over one of his men.

"Leave that coat and your weapons here," he whispered. "Then go back through the trees and come out on that trail to the right. As you get to that fork, check your shoelace. While you do that, check for any sign that the horse was there."

"Yes, Sir." The man said as he turned away.

The Mercenary waited in the shadows. He pulled out his scope to observe his man.

He also watched the fence row on the other side of the park for any sign. His man came to the fork, stumbled a bit, and looked down. He knelt as if he was tying his shoe. His head turned left and right slowly as his fingers worked the strings. After a few moments, he stood, wiped his brow, and then continued walking up the path towards the houses. He left the pavement and started walking down a dirt path that led by the back fence rows.

He waved his hand at one point as if wiping away a mosquito, then continued on the path towards the opposite tree line. The Mercenary was still worried about the lack of animal sounds... he kept his eyes on his man through his scope. His man disappeared down the path through the trees. He paused when his man didn't show up on the other side. Suddenly the birds above him started chittering. The sudden noise made him jerk his head around. The birds were disturbed by something. He wanted to look closer to see what it was but instead turned his eye back to where his man should be. He had lost sight of the tree line when the sudden noises had made him jump. His man was there when he looked again. He was heading back. The Mercenary looked at his man's face through the scope. The man's face showed success. He knew where to look. As he returned, he did not take the same path back.

Caleb had watched this man from the tree. The man had never looked up. When they got the documents, Caleb was almost sure this was one of the men at Tom's house. He wanted to see where this man would go. When the man returned to the tree line across from the safe house, Caleb saw the Mercenary for a moment. He knew they were too far for him to get to them where they were. He moved down the tree and backed away to keep himself hidden. He couldn't go to Frank. That would confirm for them exactly where to find the safe house. When he was sure they wouldn't see, he went back to Gray and mounted. He turned away and headed the long way around till he reached a trail back into the park. He rode out of the tree line and stopped.

He waited long enough to be sure the Mercenary had seen him. Then he turned Gray back into the trees at a gallop. He would give Frank the time he needed. After a short way without slowing down, he dropped the reins, stood in the saddle, and caught a branch. He swung up onto the branch and whistled a command to Gray. Gray kept going around the next two turns in the path, then stopped and stepped into the trees. Gray went around a thicket of hedges and stood silently with his head down.

Caleb climbed up a few more branches and sat waiting.

The Mercenary sent half a squad around the park trails to the left. He sent the other half across the park, following his earlier man's path. He radioed Thompson to take his entire squad of men around the park through the town to enter the woods on the other side to set up a perimeter to pen them in.

Thompson replied, "Do you want us to go into the woods and meet up with you in the middle?"

"No, just make sure no one slips out or comes in from that end. Can you handle that?" The Mercenary said.

"Acknowledged," Thompson replied while thinking 'fucking asshole, easy paycheck though' He then moved his men out to set up the perimeter on the other side of the woods.

The Mercenary's man had told of the house where the horse's prints had shown they had stepped off the path and stood for a time before moving on. This was something to check. For now, he wanted the old man. He remained behind his tree and observed through his binoculars. He watched his men casually execute the maneuvers to catch up to and capture the old man. The Mercenary told them he wanted the old man alive. They would obey. His men going through the trees signaled they were ready. He gave the men in the park the signal to proceed and radioed Thompson to watch from the far side of the woods to keep anyone from escaping. They had to have him trapped now.

Caleb waited. He knew they would try to pen him in. He was cautious. Their weapons would have more range than his revolvers, but they would have less advantage in close quarters in the trees. He un-flapped his Colts holsters and loosened the Remington pistols in their holsters. He was as ready as he was going to be.

The men passed the horse without realizing it. They moved slowly and as they neared the spot. Soon, they pulled their guns. Caleb watched. He saw them pass underneath him and waited. He had the bow ready, but they were too close. He would never be able to shoot and then get to his gun from here. He saw them meet up with their companions. He listened to them.

"Dammit, where did he go?"

"Hell if I know."

"We were too slow; he may have gone out towards the roadway back there."

"Head back and tell the boss that we are going to pursue him. We'll pin him back against Thompson's squad. They better not let anyone slip out of these trees."

The one turned to head back; the rest headed up the trail. None of them noticed Caleb above them. He let them go. After there were no other sounds, he climbed down. Two clicks of his tongue and Gray came around the hedges.

"Go back to Frank," he said. "I'll be along shortly."

Gray turned from the path and headed through the trees to the safe house. He stopped in the tree line out of sight but could still see the house. Gray saw the Merc approaching the back of the house. He could tell this man was dangerous. He felt the need to hide but also was driven to protect his herd. One of his new herd was within the house this strange man was approaching. Gray quietly moved out of the trees behind this man. As the man stalked closer to the house's back door, Gray stalked him; padding onto the soft lawn through the gate the man had left open. The man had avoided the windows not to be seen by those inside.

Gray had different intentions. He stepped in plain sight of the window. He shook his head and caught Frank's attention, then pointed with his nose at the man at the back door. He then turned back through the gate and quickly ran back into the woods, making much more noise.

The Mercenary rounded the corner and spotted one of his men approaching the old man's horse. Before he could do anything, the beast reared up and lashed out with a hoof, striking the man on the head. In a moment, the horse was gone, and the wounded man lay on the ground.

"Dammit," the Merc said, rushing forward. He knelt to check his man. There was nothing he could do. He had lost another man. "That bastard and his damn horse are both going down."

He stood and continued down the path. Suddenly the quiet of the woods was disturbed by the staccato of gunfire and men yelling. He started running towards the sounds. He came upon his men firing into the trees. Two more of his men were down, leaving the three remaining in a retreating maneuver covering for each other as they were fighting like hell to put distance between themselves and their enemy. He could not see who was firing back at them, but a slow, steady report was coming from around the corner. Another man went down. He was hit in the leg and kept crawling toward the tree line the other men had reached.

Suddenly there were no more shots coming their way. He reached his men and ordered them to cease fire.

"What the hell happened?" he yelled.

"We followed the path to verify the target had not left the woods, Sir. Thompson's men are still out there, and they said nobody came out that way. When we came back, we watched for him, and a few joggers came around the corner. Fucking Thompson didn't turn them away. We stopped them; you know we can't have witnesses. We tied them and led them back off the path. We were ready to take care of them when we started taking fire. We couldn't get a clear shot and had to retreat. Mueller tried to take care of the joggers, and he was dropped. A single shot through his eye."

The Merc looked at the men he had left here. He grabbed his secure radio. "All units… We are done. All of you disperse, head back out, and withdraw. This job ain't worth all this bullshit. Thompson, get your worthless team out of there." He never heard Thompson's reply as he had shifted channels with his men by protocol.

He turned to his men here. "You guys, with me, we are going to clean this mess up, and then you guys bug out too." The Merc wasn't going to risk his men anymore. They were out. Damn the money. His men were worth more than this—But he would stay. That old man was going to pay. The Merc was going to take care of him personally.

His men hesitated a moment, then went forward to recover their fallen. No further shots were coming their way.

19

Caleb

Caleb had watched the mercenaries; he wanted to stay hidden and escape them without bloodshed. However, as they came through, they had encountered people on the path. He had watched until he saw what they intended. He couldn't allow it. Before they could perform the task, he had both colts out. His first shots were simultaneous shots from his left and right hand. The two men who were closest to the unfortunate people fell over. Then he turned his guns at the remaining men and fired first one hand then the other keeping their heads down. The people who were about to be victims had taken off through the trees; they would be safe soon enough. One man tried to pursue. Caleb took him with a shot that passed through his right temple and out his left eye. The people were safe. The mercenaries were now turning their weapons on him.

The tree he was behind had a thick trunk, and they couldn't get him. He just kept firing slowly and steadily around the tree. He hit another, and they started backing out. He pursued several steps keeping up his firing. As his colts ran out of ammo, he holstered them and pulled the Remington in such a smooth motion that there was no pause in his shooting. The men were almost around the corner when he hit another. He fired his last shots in the trees next to these men, then stopped and simply walked straight away, hidden from them by the thick trees. As he walked, he reloaded. When he reached the second path, there was Gray. Caleb noticed the bloody hoof, checked the big horse for injuries, then nodded at Gray and mounted up.

"Back to Frank," he said.

Gray turned through the trees and headed directly to the safe house; Caleb continued reloading on the way, trusting Gray to get him where they were going. They met up with Frank as he was about to enter the woods. He had heard the gunfire and had called it in. He was going to go in alone when Caleb and Gray appeared in front of him. Caleb reached down, took his hand, and again quickly swung Frank up behind him. Then they were off across the park at full speed.

They were at the trees when the Mercenary came out of the path behind them. He saw them disappear; he wished he had the motorcycle with him. He heard the sirens and disappeared back through the trees. His men were already gone. He would be hunting that Old Man again soon enough, but he couldn't afford to be caught here now.

He disappeared through the trees, moving in a different direction. He cut across the paths not seen by anyone. At the end of the woods, he found the old pickup his men had left for him. Exit strategies were as vital to him as the plan of attack. Neither he nor his men would ever be stuck somewhere with no means of getting out. He climbed into the cab and headed back to his base. When he arrived, he found his men caring for the wounded. They had already taken care of the dead. When they were finished, he ordered all his squads and informed them that they were no longer on this job. It was not worth the number of men he had lost. He ordered them to head out of the state and stay clear till they heard from him. He watched as they all left, going their own ways. When he was alone again, he began thinking hard. What had gone wrong? He had the best men at what they do. He chose his teams and cycled through them, and changed out teams as needed. He had been involved in many operations and never had this much trouble. It was maddening. This was just a quick job that should have been one or two days of work. After his men were gone, he locked up and left himself. He did not leave town as he had told his men. No, he was not leaving quite yet. He climbed into his truck and drove back towards the mountain. He would find that old man.

20

Jamison

Frank was sitting at a patio table out in front of the café, drinking a cup of coffee. He was wearing a torn shirt and a hoodie over his head, hanging down over his forehead. His sunglasses were oversized and covered most of his face. His three-day beard and disheveled clothing made him nearly unrecognizable. Ward Jamison walked across the café patio, sat behind Frank, and ordered coffee and a ham and egg sandwich. Anyone looking at this café would never suspect that these men knew each other, let alone were having a conversation. How they were conversing was highly classified. They were sure they would not be intercepted as they worked on a proprietary set of radio channels utilizing multiple random frequency hopping algorithms between them. Only the two small radios in their ears were in range of each other. They would be out of range if they moved six inches further away. Frank relayed to Jamison the location of the jump drives and the names he had figured out from the list. He knew Jamison would be able to clear up the rest. He also told Jamison about the Mercenary. Jamison asked if the Mercenary had any identifying marks to help with researching just who he was. Frank relayed what few marks and scars he noticed. He also told of the methods and tactics he recognized from how the Mercenary's team operated. Jamison did not indicate having heard anything of use; he just paid for his meal and coffee when the waitress dropped it off. She stepped to Frank next; he thanked her, paid for his meal, left a generous tip, then rose and walked away with a noticeable limp.

From the description Frank gave, Jamison suspected he knew the Mercenary; it seemed to be someone he knew who was called in from time to time. Jamison began to be concerned. This man and his team were a problem since going independent. They were hacking into classified data and selling their services and data to the highest bidder. If this was the Mercenary Jamison knew, he was on two lists. The first was as an asset to be used when the US could not officially have anything to do with an operation. The second list was for potential elimination in the likely event that the US Government needed to avoid embarrassing diplomatic events.

Jamison was not sure of his suspicions. This was far out of character for the man he knew, but he had to admit there was something there when presented with the description. He did not know; it seemed solid, but he didn't think the man he knew would have taken a job that would have the potential to be this public. Even if he had, Jamison did not think it would be possible for them to have failed this many times to complete the task; he was that good. Maybe some of his team would make mistakes like this but not him.

Jamison finished his meal and left a 20-dollar bill on the table. He walked away, and as he was stepping down to the sidewalk, he stumbled and dropped his case on the lawn. It popped open and spilled some of the contents. He started picking everything up, dropped his radio earpiece in the case, and picked up several documents and jump drives that had spilled out. No one noticed anything strange, even the tail that was on him. Jamison relocked his case and looked at the clasp as if trying to figure out why it had opened. He shook his case, and the clip opened. Jamison held it down and stepped into an office supply store. He picked out a new case and then paid at the counter.

He started moving everything from the old case into the new one. No one would notice that there were more jump drives than he started with. Then he left the store, walking down the street, sensing that he was being followed. He turned into the parking lot, climbed into his car, and nearly bumped into the tail as he was leaving. He was looking in the opposite direction at traffic, so the man could not suspect Jamison had detected him. When Jamison turned back and saw him there, he waved an apology and pulled away. Jamison knew he had confirmed the tail and that the tail had missed the transfer. Jamison left, and he was back at his office before anyone could suspect anything other than a brief lunch break had taken place.

21

The Arrow, Memories

Caleb was sitting at the table fitting an ancient arrowhead to a new shaft. He had carefully peeled the bark from a willow branch and sanded it smooth. He had meticulously worked the pole over a fire to straighten it as much as possible. This he did more by feel than by sight. He would roll the shaft on his arm till he felt it move smoothly. He then notched the end and held the arrowhead in place. He wound the sinew strips around the arrowhead, fitting it into the notch.

He carefully adjusted his technique to ensure the winding did not have any gaps. He had also used sinew to fasten the feathers to the shaft. When he was satisfied, he pulled the knots tight. As the ligament dried, it would tighten further. He had been at this for an hour waiting for Frank to return. He was covering the sinew with a layer of pitch he had boiled down over the fire. This would ensure the windings would not slip or come loose. When he was finished, he set the new arrow down next to the old arrows. Other than the shaft not being tarnished by the many hands touching it over the past years, the new arrow looked very similar to the others. Caleb smiled. He had never done this before, but the memory was in him. He had been working without thought as if someone else was working the shaft. He gathered them back up and placed them in the quiver.

Frank walked into the cabin and spoke. "It's done now. I turned it all over. We have to let Jamison work this now."

Caleb nodded. "We should wait here for a bit."

Frank was peeling off the disguise he had used. He turned back to Caleb.

"Why? Shouldn't we be getting back to protect the kids as soon as possible?"

"Not just yet," Caleb stated quietly. "First, you need to tell me more about these soldiers I was fighting." Frank turned to him fully. He was surprised at the question. He had come to think that Caleb already knew about them.

Caleb saw the confusion momentarily flash across Frank's face and said, "I have dealt with soldiers and mercenaries before, but these weapons are impressive. I was—" Caleb paused for a moment, "unprepared for their firepower."

"I will tell you what I can."

Caleb asked several questions about the weaponry these Mercenaries had at their disposal. He did not think he could face that gunfire again. He had to admit to himself he was surprised at the speed the guns could fire and reload. Frank showed him his service weapon. He explained the function and also explained the rifles the other soldiers were carrying. The fully automatic weapons had concerned Caleb. He had been able to subdue the men in the woods near the park but did not believe he would be able to face them in the open. Frank and he began to work on new plans. They would stay away from the kids and the Chief as long as possible. No sense risking that in they were being followed. In the end, Caleb asked Frank to get one or two of these weapons for him. He would like to see what they were capable of to better prepare for the next time. Caleb thought to himself that they would be an excellent addition to his collection.

They ate a meal in silence, then slipped out into the night. Frank was going to meet again with Ward. Caleb did not say where he was going, only that he needed to go up the mountain.

22

The Mercenary

The Mercenary was sitting at the desk listening to the office noises. People were walking by, talking in the hallway. He was alone in the office, the blinds keeping the outside light from entering the room. The door opened and closed as the man flipped the light switch on. He started at the sight of the Mercenary casually sitting there.

The Merc spoke quietly. "Sir, I am pulling my men out of this job. I have lost too many because you did not give me all the information I needed." The other man reached for the door and froze when the Merc suddenly had the weapon pointed at him. "Don't do that," he said.

The man was turning red with anger. "You're backing out? That is not an option. We already paid you."

"I didn't say I was backing out; I just pulled my men out. And here is my report and your fucking money if you want it!" the Mercenary growled and tossed the folder and bag on the floor. "Less the cost of taking care of my injured and dead men. They died because you failed to give me all the information I needed about these targets. Now you are going to fill me in on it *all*. Then, I will complete this for you myself."

The man stepped into the room and sat at the chair usually reserved for those visiting him in his office.

"What didn't we give you? You had addresses, habits, and schedules. It's not my fault your men fucked up." The man paused, staring back into the Merc's eyes. "You had everything I had. What was so hard about this job? You said it was a matter of timing and simple enough."

"Well," said the Merc, "someone, shall we say, tipped off the Feds that a hit was coming down. They were on the scene before completing the task and almost before we could get out of there. I was assured all targets were at the location. They weren't there. I was also not informed that they have some sort of personal guard unit that is professional. So you either didn't have all the information you said you had or you double-crossed me."

The Merc continued speaking, "Now, I am trying to decide if you set me up or are just incompetent. Either way, I don't like working with you," the Merc glared at the man and continued, "you need a new contact."

The man stood up. "You think you can talk to me that way? You aren't supposed to be contacting me anyway!" he yelled. Then he slammed his hand on the desk next to the phone. An emergency light began flashing in the hallway.

The Merc saw him hit the alarm and calmly stood up and stepped around the desk. He walked over to the door and listened to the sounds of men running down the hall.

He turned back to the man and asked in a cold voice. "Do you really think there is anyone in this building that can stop me?"

The man stiffened as the Merc calmly walked across the room again, never moving his weapon from pointing directly at the man's face. Then the Merc stepped behind the blinds, through the window, and out on the ledge just as the security guards burst through the door.

There was a loud bang as the small charge next to the door went off. The men storming the room were knocked to the floor, partially stunned and momentarily blinded, as was the man.

The Merc calmly stepped back in off the ledge and picked up the bag of money.

He spoke to the man whose ears were ringing so bad it was difficult to hear. "I will finish this job, but after this, don't you ever call me again." Then the Merc walked out the door of the office. He exited with the rest of the people as the building's intercom was announcing the emergency exit. On the way to the front he avoided cameras and where he couldn't avoid the guards, they were found unconscious but otherwise uninjured, as if he didn't think they were worth the effort to kill. The Merc was gone before the man could even find his way out of his office.

The Merc knew the gravity of what he had done. This man was not one to be trifled with. Harder badasses than the Mercenary had been taken down by him. He would have to play it smart to survive.

23

The Chief's Cabin

The Chief and Annie were out in the woods. They told Sarah and Tom that the Chief would be giving Annie instructions in natural medicine if they needed first aid. They were near enough that they could return at a moment's notice but far enough that he could give Annie her lessons in private. He taught her how to find the herbs and roots needed for remedies; also what natural minerals would help in healing. He was also teaching Annie of Maribel and her line of mystics as well. He told her of how Maribel had discovered these talents at a young age and been taught how to read the insights and feelings of others. Maribel had been tactile. She could read someone by touching them or an object they had held. The Chief told Annie that she had the same gift. He could begin her training and find someone to continue when they were free of the current situation. He showed her how to read these feelings and how to focus, to begin to understand the sensations when she felt them. She was amazed as he was teaching her. She had always had these feelings but had no idea why. She had thought that she imagined it all before the

Chief began to explain. He taught her what to focus on initially to start to control the sensations. She often would sense many different feelings that were contradictory. The Chief showed her how she was reading multiple people at the same time. He taught her how she was able to sense some communication from animals. This was how Gray was able to respond to her so well. She could understand his feelings and project her thoughts to him without even knowing she did so. Their first session lasted over two hours. The time flew by so fast that she didn't realize it until the Chief called a halt.

"Time to return," he said. "We have to take care of the horses and start preparing supper."

Annie thought a moment. "Do you think we gave them enough time?"

The Chief laughed. "Your insight is quite accurate. I believe so, but we will be sure to announce our arrival with enough time for them to avoid embarrassment."

The Chief then handed her a necklace. It was handmade by him and it held the charm he had taken from Maribel. "I am sure now that this is to be yours. With this, your skills will be enhanced. Keep it with you near your heart."

She looked at the little charm closely. It was beautiful yet simple. She placed the necklace over her head. "Thank you," she said quietly. She could feel the charm held some power, almost electric. The tingling sensation on her hand and her chest was like the after-effects of being shocked but with no pain. It actually felt natural.

The Chief watched her carefully. He could tell she felt the charge. He was assured that she was the one. He was very thankful to the spirits for having led him to her so quickly after Maribel. He would refer to her now as Lady Annie. He thought of who he would need to contact to help with her training. Lady Maribel had been one of the last, but there were others he knew. It would take some time to contact them and see if they would take an apprentice now that the woman was gone. Some would want to take Maribel's essence into their own power. To find the correct mentor, he would have to search carefully.

As they returned to the cabin, they gathered hay and apples and then picked up the grain sack from next to the house. The Chief was sure to bang the grain bin lid just loud enough to be heard inside the cabin. Then he and Annie went through the tree line back over to the horses. As they took care of the horses, Annie asked, "Do you think Sarah knows she loves him yet?"

The Chief thought for a moment. "Maybe she does, Lady Annie, but perhaps she doesn't wish to admit it yet. She may fear losing him now would be too painful if she loved him."

"Then we shall not press the matter."

The Chief approved her decision; he was impressed with her maturity for one so young. She impressed him more and more. He would be proud to have her as a granddaughter. At that moment, Sarah came out of the cabin. Her hair was straight, and she looked only slightly flushed. She went through the trees and began to help comb the horses.

"Hi," she said, "did you have a good lesson?"

Annie told her of the herbs and roots that would help heal minor injuries and illnesses. She showed Sarah some of the items they gathered and asked Sarah if she would like to help prepare them for storage to be ready if needed. Sarah was happy to do so.

Tom came out of the cabin looking a little unkempt. He had showered and dressed quickly. As he looked around, he saw Sarah and Annie talking. He smiled nervously and walked over through the tree line to join them.

The Chief met him at the corner of the corral and handed him the rake and shovel. "Let's go clean up the bedding for the horses."

Tom was grateful that there was something for him to do that would take much concentration. He knew he would be distracted as his thoughts went back to his afternoon. He had not anticipated Sarah would have been ready to go so far with him. He had been surprised and nervous. She only said that they both needed this. She asked him not to put too much meaning into it. She just needed something real for a moment to take her away from the fear of the last few days.

As he and the Chief worked, he kept glancing over at Sarah. He was a little concerned about what Annie would say if she knew. Annie had told him he wasn't good enough for Sarah, but Annie was changing before his eyes. The little girl he knew from just a few weeks ago was gone. She seemed to be so much more now. He worried about her. His thoughts turned inward as he began to blame himself. If he hadn't hacked those computers, the family would never have had to flee. As he thought of that, he realized he would have never met Sarah. His thoughts were running together when the Chief put his hand on his shoulder.

"You are not to blame for this. This burden was thrust upon you due to what others have done," said the Chief.

Tom looked into the Chief's eyes. The depth and understanding in the older man's eyes were calming. Tom was able to pull back from his torturous thoughts and return to the present. "Thank you," he said. Then he and the Chief continued cleaning the horse shelter and laying down new straw for them.

The Chief spread a powder over the straw and raked it in. "This will keep ticks and biting flies away at night so the horses can rest.

24

Caleb's Doubt

Caleb and Gray entered the clearing. The stream was there and the cave. Caleb sat on the rock next to the opening, closed his eyes, and thought of the Irishman.

"I need to know," he said.

"Well, what ya need to know," came the response.

"When is it enough? I am caring about these kids. I don't think I can take it if I lose one of them. How will I carry the pain of the loss if I fail them? I already failed their parents by arriving too slowly. I failed Lady Maribel; I should have gone with the Chief. She, too, is gone because of my failure."

"You're not to blame. You were called for the children. They are the ones who need you. Lady Maribel did not; it was just her time. She knew her time was comin' an' she chose to protect the girl with the time she had left. It was her choice, and she is celebrated for it beyond. You are not to blame for her passing. The parents are not your burden to bear; they were never your charge. Their loss is tragic, but you have kept their family line alive. That was your duty, your mission. You have done right by them. Now go, do as you are meant, Chosen."

Caleb opened his eyes. He was alone in the clearing. His mind was still churning, and he still felt the sting of those deaths, but his mind was clear. He stood and called Gray over, mounted, and left the clearing.

Though Caleb couldn't see him, the Irishman was there. He was sitting on the rock next to where Caleb had been. As Caleb left, he stood and walked back into the cave; it began to close behind him, and he paused. He turned towards the woods. Someone was there, and he felt it. He moved back out of the cave and stepped away as the trees closed in and the clearing disappeared again.

25

The Report

Jamison was in the briefing room. His immediate superior, Director Jim Forrester, and the Directors of the other organizations were arguing about the case. He had just finished his report. He had detailed that there was a mercenary group that was involved. He did not have any hard evidence of who they were yet. He had presented the evidence of the man who had exposed the Langston family and revealed the safe house. He was tracking down the sources of the payments that had been discovered while investigating this man. He did not tell them that he suspected there were more within the organization that had been turned. He watched them. He was looking for any subtle clue to show if one of these men was involved.

Jim Forrester was defending Frank Johnston, stating almost word for word what Jamison had told him.

The man next to Forrester slammed his hand on the table. "I don't care if you think he is golden boy number one; his witnesses were killed on his watch. His team was wiped out, and we have had no communication with him. He is either involved, or he's dead along with the witnesses he had left!"

This hothead is a worthless waste of breath, thought Jamison. "I know Frank Johnston hasn't turned. I also know he is alive as well as his witnesses." Jamison glared at the man named Martin Wells. "Johnston is the one who reported the Mercenary involvement and found the phone records showing how the Langstons were betrayed from this very building. He is not a suspect in this. Unless you have real proof, stop wasting our time."

Wells glared back at him.

Another one to take down a step, he thought.

"As long as *you* are sure, I guess we can let that matter rest for now," he said. The implication that Wells was going to proceed with an investigation into Frank Johnston was not very subtly implied, but Jamison let it pass to move on.

The meeting went on for another hour. When they left, they had a plan of action. They needed to find the mercenary and arrest him if he were still alive. They had to find out who brought him in. They would send the remaining documentation that Jamison had presented and break the code to determine how many people were involved and possibly identify them.

Jamison had kept back several documents from the meeting that could have possibly involved one or two men in this meeting. He didn't want to take the risk that they would suspect he was investigating them. He was hoping that he could flush out the traitor by reviewing this meeting tape. He had his suspicions but needed to be sure before proceeding. In addition to the recordings, he had also baited a trap in the meeting. He let slip some false leads as to the whereabouts of the witnesses. Only he and Jim Forrester knew the incorrect information that was presented. If that information was passed along, they would know one of the men in the meeting was involved.

It seemed Jamison had inadvertently revealed the location where Frank Johnston was hiding the kids by requesting an additional support team to protect the area of a safe house. Unknown to these men, he had sent a team to set up the safe place in the city. It would appear that this location had the routine surveillance that would be expected when hiding a priority target. He did not reveal that there was an additional layer of surveillance. The hidden cameras were backed up with redundant systems presenting multiple angles. This location would have more than twice the usual number of cameras, many of which would be shielded and self-contained to prevent hacking. This had all been set up before this meeting with the idea to capture whoever was sent to go after the safe house. They only had to wait to see if anyone tried infiltrating this wrong location. It was now a waiting game.

26

The Mercenary

The Mercenary had followed the old man up the mountain. He needed to know more about this adversary. What kind of fight was he in this time? He had kept his distance from the cabin. He had seen Frank Johnston arrive and saw the men in deep discussion. He waited and observed, then watched both men leave. He knew the children were not there, so he would have to follow these men to find them. He had hesitated to decide which of the men to follow but only for a moment. The opportunity to get the old man alone was too much to face in that moment.

He had cautiously kept out of sight as he climbed the trails behind the old man and the horse. The old man seemed troubled and was not hiding his path. At first, this gave the Mercenary a more straightforward track to follow, but as the man and the horse got further ahead of him, the trail faded quickly. If the Mercenary had not been following from the start and known the older man was alone and just ahead of him, he would have sworn he had lost the trail. It seemed as if he was following a day-old, then a week-old track. Suddenly, the path was gone.

The mercenary backtracked to the last spot he was sure he had seen the signs of the horse passing. All he found were his own tracks. He looked about, trying to make sure he was not missing something. He saw the ridge ahead and climbed to get a better view. As he topped the rise, he saw the old man entering a clearing across the narrow valley, not more than five hundred meters away. He pulled his scope up to try to judge the distance the man had traveled, and he could not see the clearing through the scope. He dropped it down; without the scope, he could see where the old man had entered the clearing.

He could see the old man sitting next to a cave opening, but when the Mercenary looked through the scope, there were only trees; no horse, no man, no cave—not even a clearing. He dropped the scope back into his pack. He watched the scene across the narrow gap, and it seemed there was a shadow next to the old man.

The old man appeared broken, hunched down, and weary. But eventually, he seemed to pull himself together and stand. The old man looked around the small clearing, mounted his horse, and left. The Mercenary watched as the old man left and the entrance through the trees into the clearing seemed to disappear.

As the old man rode away, the Mercenary watched the shadow stand; it appeared to look around and then moved into the cave. Then as the opening closed, the entire clearing closed in with dense trees.

"What the hell?"

As he started to look back to find the Old Man again, he realized he was gone. He cast about, looking for him through the trees. Suddenly a voice behind him made him jump.

"Well, Buachaill, did you see what you needed to?" followed by a laugh that faded quickly into the breeze.

The Mercenary spun around, weapon in hand, ready to defend himself. There was no one there. He kept the gun ready and slowly turned, holding it between him and where he heard the laughter moving away. Now the only sound was wind in the trees. After a few minutes, he holstered his weapon and turned to go back.

What's going on with me? I've never been jumpy like this.

He made his way back down to the main path. He would go back to his headquarters to regroup. He had to make a plan to go back to the cabin where he had first seen the girls and set up surveillance. Then he would watch and wait. Somehow he knew that from there, he would find the kids.

The Irishman had only been able to watch him. He was surprised the man had heard him, but he couldn't touch the Mercenary. The Irishman was no longer among the living. He could not venture far from the cave, and the farther he was, the less substantial he became. This was the farthest he had ever been able to go, but he could feel that he was being pulled back now. He reluctantly returned, praying that Caleb or the Chief would be able to stop this mercenary. He slid back into the cave and was gone.

27

Annie

The Chief watched Annie and Sarah from a distance. He noted how Annie was reacting to her newfound extra senses. He could tell when the insight would impose on Annie's thoughts. She would tense up, and her eyes would glass over momentarily. She was bringing herself back to reality quicker now. Soon no one would notice when she was away. Sarah had noticed a few times, and Annie would tell her some of what she saw, but sometimes the feelings were too much. She just didn't have the experience to understand the visions fully. The Chief would teach what he could, but he knew he could only take her so far. She would need to begin studying with a true mystic practitioner. He had a woman in mind if she would accept an apprentice, especially an apprentice that was not native. He would have to try to convince her.

Sarah had been worried about Annie's quiet moments and had expressed her concerns with Tom. When she asked, Annie initially told her not to worry, but as the frequency increased, so did Sarah's concern. Finally, the Chief told Annie to tell Tom and Sarah what she was training for and what it meant to see her in a trance. Annie told them more than the Chief would have allowed in typical situations. However, in their present state, he felt they had the right to know more about the training. This reduced the stress on Annie and eased her training.

28

Thompson

Martin Wells was waiting in his office. It was very late, so he and his men were the last in the office. His men were all new. The crew that had allowed his office to be infiltrated had all been re-assigned. Wells had scheduled this meeting after guessing that Jamison's request to supply additional support at the safe house meant the kids were there. He was waiting on Thompson. Wells wanted nothing further to do with his last contractor. This Thompson had been highly recommended and was known to have a bug up his ass about Roy. Wells could use that. At the knock on the door, he said: "Come."

The soldier named Thompson was escorted in by Well's new security.

"Sit," Wells said, gesturing to the chair next to the desk. "We have an issue that I need to have addressed tonight."

Thompson didn't move towards the chair; he just stood at ease in the middle of the office staring at Wells. They stared at each other for a moment. Wells was externally calm, but inside he was questioning himself. He was getting annoyed at these men who refused to show him respect. Finally, just before he was about to repeat his offer to sit, Thompson spoke:

"Thank you, Sir." He stepped over to the chair.

Before he sat, he turned back to look at the guards, "Do these men have clearance? Or is our meeting over?"

"Dismissed," said Wells as he gestured towards the door.

The guards stepped through the door and closed it. Thompson heard the automatic lock and momentarily grinned. However, the smirk was gone before he turned back to Wells. "Sir, what task do you have for my team?"

"I have two," Wells shifted in his seat and handed a packet to Thompson. "This man has been classified as a spy. He has been found to have planned cyber-attacks on this government. He has been scheduled for elimination. The problem is he has been working within our departments, and to arrest him would lead to investigations we can't afford to allow at this time. So we need him to be eliminated in a way that will not shine a light this way."

Thompson opened the cover and looked down at a face he knew well, Steve Roy's face. The Mercenary. Thompson felt a thrill, but outwardly he showed no reaction. He had worked with Roy many times, but he had only used Thompson's team and never brought him in as part of Roy's direct team. Roy had always claimed the best jobs for himself and his team. Thompson knew this would be a challenge, but it would mean he was at the top of the list when he took Roy out.

Wells handed the second packet over. "This one is a little more delicate." He waited while Thompson opened the pack. There were three kids. The boy, Tom, looked to be about 19. There were two girls. Both looked to be high school age. Wells continued talking. "We need these kids brought in. This boy has been holding the information that we need. He has been difficult to convince. We need the girls to encourage him to provide the missing documentation."

Thompson read the quick briefing on the kids. The location listed was marked as a safe house. He thought that odd but closed the packets and shoved them into an inside pocket of his shirt.

"Which is the priority?" he asked without inflection.

"Take the kids first," Wells said. "We don't know how long they will be there."

Thompson stood and walked to the door. He waited for Wells to trip the lock then stepped into the hallway. The security detail led him down the hall and out the side exit avoiding the main entrance. He disappeared into the dark.

29

The Mercenary Regroups

The Mercenary had returned to town. His mind was racing, trying to understand what he had seen. He had seen the clearing easily yet when he took his eyes off of it for a moment it was gone as if it was never there. He was also troubled by the voice he had heard; he didn't recognize it. Usually, when he heard voices it was memories of people he had met and conversations he had, but this was different. It was not someone he could remember. The voice bothered him the most.

His thoughts were interrupted by his phone buzzing in his shirt pocket. He pulled it out and glanced down as he walked. The message on his phone was nothing, just benign text to anyone who saw it. Just a stupid joke sent from a friend. The Mercenary knew at a glance there was information for him. He tapped the button on the phone to ensure it was secure. Satisfied, he clicked into the secure line and listened. He was given the coordinates and the target codes needed. He instantly memorized them, all while talking out loud as if speaking to an old friend.

He stepped off the street into the building. It looked like a normal business and indeed did have a storefront that was what appeared to be a hiking store. It was doing enough business to appear to be successful. The Mercenary slipped through the store unseen by the security cameras, knowing the pattern and timing of each sweep. He grabbed a shirt and pants and slipped unnoticed the second changing room. After a moment he hung the clothes on the middle hook and pressed the left screw. The back wall slid over silently three inches then swung back with just enough room for him to slip through. He waited for the panel to slide silently back into place as the front door of the changing room opened slightly. The stock boy walking by the changing room glanced in, saw the clothes hanging there, and took them back to the restock cart, never knowing the man hadn't come back out.

The Mercenary moved through the passage to the access stairs to this building's real purpose. His men had been dismissed and told to disperse, but the rudimentary crew was still in place, maintaining the security of his operation. The 5-man team was finishing up the lockdown of the building.

"What are your orders, Sir?" said the team leader.

"Where are we with the shutdown?" the Mercenary asked.

"The last backup was done an hour ago. We have the drives on the truck and en route. We are finishing up the secure wipe of the last systems. Your office was last."

"I will handle that. You guys get going as soon as that PC is wiped. I will contact you in a month."

"Yes Sir," the team lead turned away and barked out to the others. "You heard him. Pack it up." They moved with the efficiency of the well-practiced drill and were gone in 20 minutes, each carrying a sack of new purchases from the storefront hiding the items they were taking with them.

The Mercenary waited in his office till all were gone. He monitored them leaving, pleased that they were out and unnoticed by anyone on the street. He watched the monitors for a full hour before he opened the secure contact. He verified the coordinates with his memory of the previous message, confirmation of target, and security. He was momentarily optimistic. Then it occurred to him... This is another safe house. One safe house had already been hit and a second one had been compromised. The security around this one should be heightened and noticeably active. Everything in the documentation he was given was at the normal security levels. He rechecked the documentation. No additional measures appeared to have been taken. He thought for a moment and confirmed in his mind. This is a trap. He would proceed to verify but would be very cautious and unseen. He had to verify, but he was certain the targets were not there.

He left the shop through a different path. None of his men would know. None of them were on his team when the building was designed. None of them were aware of the additional security measures he had designed himself. It was not long before he was out and cruising the street on a Harley Street Glide. If you were not standing right next to him, you would never be able to tell this was the same man. His helmet was the smallest half helmet allowed by law and the long hair flowing out from under it flew behind him in the wind. He cruised up and down the streets as if he was just out for a ride taking random turns to avoid having to stop and put his feet down, always giving the down low wave to other bikers, sometimes the two-finger peace sign about level with his hip, sometimes an open hand with his palm forward. His smile was that of a man with no care in the world enjoying the ride. In reality, his thoughts were focused, and he was very alert. He knew he had passed three unmarked cars and one van he had identified as surveillance vehicles. He confirmed the trap but still rode closer to the target house. As he rode past he recognized Frank in the old hobo disguise. Not everyone would have recognized him, but the Mercenary had memorized those eyes. He knew he had been set up and now he had to figure out by who.

The Mercenary rode on and disappeared down the street. He parked the Harley in a mall lot near the security shack. Before he walked away, he opened the saddlebag, pulled out a spray bottle, and lovingly polished the bike to a bright shine. Then he wiped the bottle down and returned it to the bag. He locked the bike, waved to the guard at the shack, and walked into the mall. He stopped in a public restroom. Minutes later he emerged from a different door dressed in shorts and a loud Hawaiian shirt; the hair was gone. He stepped into a bar in the mall and ordered a margarita and sat in a booth. When he finished his drink, he went out to the other end of the mall walking away with a crowd of people leaving the movie theater.

Within a half-hour of his escape, the Police received a report that a Harley Street Glide reported stolen earlier that day had been found in the Mall parking lot. By the time they had checked the bike, the Mercenary was gone. The freshly polished bike shone in the sun as if it had been professionally detailed, with no fingerprints to be found.

30

Thompson

Thompson took his time; his recon of the safe house had shown the security details he expected, plus the additional unmarked security vehicles he had been warned of by Wells. He sent his man to verify the targets were in the house and confirmed via thermal scans that three people, one young man, and two young women, were guarded there. He then sent the infiltration squad he had hired around back to start taking out the security measures. These were not his men. He had chosen them and told them the entire time they were being briefed on the task that they were working for Steve Roy. He had made sure they were aware of this as often as possible. Now today, he was sending them in to retrieve the targets. He knew if any of them went down, they would implicate Roy. He kept his men with him in his command truck.

His command truck was a moving van. To anyone walking by, it appeared as if they were delivering furniture. His men had intercepted the wireless camera feeds in the safe house and set up the loop, so this new team would not be seen approaching. This new infiltration team then went in, hiding where they could and could breach the back of the house. He monitored from the safety of his truck.

His regular team was with him, and they continued unloading the furniture they delivered to the old lady's home. It was convenient scheduling to have found this delivery on the same block, and he was proud of his cleverness hiding in plain sight of the safe house. While the guards were watching the delivery, he monitored the infiltration team entering the house and moving toward the target.

31

The Safe House

Frank had seen the motorcycle go past. He noted the plate number for later, but the rider had not even looked over towards the house. Next, Frank took note of the delivery truck across the street. He recognized the name of the store.

Great, he thought, *more interference.*

He stepped back into the house and changed out of the disguise into his regular clothes. He then stepped into the room with the video feeds. He watched the delivery men carry the large sofa into the house across the street.

"They don't seem to be the quality of delivery men that store usually employs. So keep an eye on them as well." He said to the man monitoring the site.

"Sir, we have a hit." was the reply.

Frank turned back to him and looked from his face to the screens. The main monitors were showing nothing. However, his backup systems showed the mercenary team moving through the yard. "Someone has looped our video, sir. I should have caught that sooner."

"No, you caught it in plenty of time. Can you get their

frequency?" Frank asked.

"Have it already, sir."

Frank nodded his approval. "OK, patch our team in. Tranquilizer guns only, and be ready to jam that signal." Frank started to walk away and paused a moment. "Don't jam them immediately; wait long enough that whoever is monitoring them knows they were caught. Then, we may flush them out too."

Satisfied his man would carry out the task as ordered, Frank turned and joined his men waiting for the assault team. The house had been set up to have forced the entire attack team to come through the small hallway after entering the structure. Thus, they would hear the kids in the room up the hall but would not see the men waiting there.

Thompson was anticipating his success in the moving truck as he watched the men enter the house; his plan was working perfectly. The team moved down the hallway in a classic infiltration pattern. Then it all went south. Before they reached the end of the hallway, their man at the door slumped against the wall and slid down onto his ass. Then, as several turned to see the dart in his neck, they were struck as well. It took 15 seconds, and a majority of the team was down. The remaining two attempted to make a quick exit only to be darted and knocked senseless.

The men had only been in the house long enough to close the door behind them when they suddenly started dropping.

Johnston's security man had performed admirably, and as the first several men had gone down, he made sure the broadcast on the body cameras remained up for 10 seconds, then the feeds were cut off. "That ought to get 'em riled up," he said as he hit the jamming switch. Frank now had an 8-

man team to question. And their employer would know they were captured. He hoped this would panic them into making a mistake.

Back in the moving van, Thompson stared at the screens. His wireless feed to the team's body cameras was cut. He had no way of knowing what was happening to them. He felt as if the floor dropped from under him. Everything had seemed to be going perfectly. He hesitated a few seconds, seething in confused anger before he used the radio in the truck to call his men dropping off the furniture.

"Hey guys, we have more deliveries today. Step it up," Thompson said.

"Yeah, boss, she wants us to move it back to the other side of the room," was the reply.

"Well, get it done, and let's go." He told them.

This was the signal they didn't want to hear. They knew their team was down. Even then, they didn't rush; they just placed the couch where the old lady said and then had her sign the papers. They closed up the truck ramp and climbed into the cab, the whole time bad-mouthing the old lady for making them move the couch several times, then just drove off, leaving their infiltration team behind.

32

Caleb's Plan

Caleb was back at the cabin, waiting for word from Frank. He was still worried about completing his task, but he was much relieved to learn that he was not called for the parents. The kids were safe; he had checked with the Chief before returning to the cabin. The kids did not know he had been there. He needed to work on a solution for their safety. He was reviewing in his mind the tactics and reactions the mercenary team had used. He was impressed by their efficiency but had been able to take advantage of terrain more suited to his experiences. He knew that would not always be the case, and he wanted to be more prepared for them. He was drawing out a map of the area surrounding the cabin and the mountain, using it to plot out the movements of the Mercenaries and find a way to gain an edge. He remembered hearing that all great fighters looked for an advantage; he needed one now. The responsibility for these children was growing the more time he spent worrying about them. He was developing almost fatherly or rather more grandfatherly feelings for them. He began missing the opportunities to have been a father himself.

While at this task, he heard the motorcycle in the distance. He stiffened momentarily till he heard it continue.

Not the same bike, he thought.

He continued planning his perimeter. He knew that the Mercenaries knew of this cabin and that they had been inside it. This made his task even more difficult. He would need to regain the advantage by adding some surprises in the woods for anyone not coming up the main trails. His plans were made, and he stepped out to begin setting up. He first scanned the area to ensure he was alone, as there was no need to be seen building the traps.

Caleb met Frank as he was pulling up the trail. Their eyes met as Frank passed by. The simple hand gesture indicated Frank should continue on to the next trail back to the cabin. Caleb then stepped back into the trees to continue his tasks.

Frank was riding up the trail on an electric ATV rigged to run very quietly. He had a large pack on the luggage rack for the old man. The men he had captured provided several modern weapons. Frank had confiscated their weapons and had not cataloged the ones in this pack. He took some from each man and built this pack to be a complete set for Caleb. He didn't feel comfortable breaking protocol, but this was a necessary deviation from his normal ethical behavior. Caleb needed these weapons to allow him to prepare for what was heading their way.

The trail Frank took came down behind the cabin, invisible from the ridge. Anyone looking at the place from the opening to the clearing would not see him. Frank had turned, coasted down silently, and parked the ATV behind the woodpile, further hiding it. He carried the pack in to await Caleb.

Caleb finished his preparations setting branches to trip,

make noise or even whip out and injure anyone coming from one of the hidden approaches to the cabin. He was satisfied that his work would not be visible to a casual observer during the day and would be nearly invisible at night, even in the brightest moonlight. If someone approached during the day, they might see signs if they knew what to look for. He felt the average man wouldn't see them unless they were trained. This worried him. That was why he made the noisemakers and whips. These were easier to hide and would give away anyone approaching. He headed back to the cabin through the woods. At one point, the timber rattler shook its tail at him, but he ignored it. It did not strike; it had a sense that to attack this man meant death. After Caleb passed, the snake moved further into the trees. It was afraid of that man.

Caleb entered the cabin and greeted Frank. Frank asked after the kids and was relieved to hear they were still well. He insisted Caleb not tell him where they were yet as there was too significant a risk. Caleb nodded then looked at the table. The weapons were arranged for viewing; some were disassembled as Frank was cleaning them. Caleb joined him, and they discussed the guns as they dismantled and cleaned the remaining weapons and then reassembled them. Frank instructed Caleb in the finer points of the mechanisms as he had instructed recruits. Caleb absorbed the information quicker and more thoroughly than any cadet ever had. Frank walked Caleb through the use of each weapon, unloaded at first so he would be familiar, then showed him how to load the magazines: 15 rounds each magazine and a couple of 30-round magazines. He also had three automatic pistols with multiple 9-round magazines for each. After going through these, Frank brought out the flash-bang stun grenades. These interested Caleb, and he asked how many were available. He wanted to place some in his traps. There were enough. They discussed the men that had been captured. Frank told him that they all reported that they were working under contract. They all indicated the same man, Steve Roy. Frank spoke with Caleb about all the information he had uncovered about Steve Roy.

Caleb was impressed by the man's credentials. Knowing his adversary was good, and could give him the edge he required.

33

Ward Jamison

Ward Jamison was going over the transcripts of the captured men's testimony. The indications that they were working for Steve Roy were compelling. All of them believed that they were operating under Roy's orders. Jamison had talked to Frank himself, and Frank described the motorcycle that went by right before the infiltration team came in; the license plate had been from a stolen bike that had been reported stolen and later recovered. From the description of the rider, Jamison was convinced that Roy was involved but not enough so to release that fact to the public. He was still troubled by the unprofessionalism of the men that were on the mission. He knew Steve Roy was much too efficient to have failed to see this was a trap. Also, the men he hired would never have revealed their commanding officer's name.

However, with all the men on that team indicating Roy was giving the orders, Jamison had to agree to Wells' demands that they go after Roy immediately. Jamison did not get the feeling that Wells was going to keep the agreement to keep their findings secret.

He did not want to assign his own people to this task. He knew Roy and did not want to be responsible for sending his own people into that much danger. He argued with Wells that due to the sensitivity of the operation, they would not want an official team going in. He convinced Wells that if an official team failed on this type of mission, it would reflect poorly on Wells himself. Wells had to agree. Jamison asked for a recommendation from Wells and was surprised how quickly it was suggested to assign this to Thompson's team. He documented all this in his official notes. He then passed on the orders.

Thompson provided no outward reaction when he was contacted to undertake this task. Internally he was ecstatic. He was now officially given the green light to go after Roy. This was his chance to end that man's monopoly on the high pay assignments. He began calling in his team again. They would be ready in the morning and quickly be on their way.

34

Steve Roy

Steve Roy had returned to his building. The shop was closed, and all customers and employees had gone home. He entered quietly through the main office door. He went immediately to his office. He opened his computer and entered the coordinates of the old man's cabin.

Next, he ran a topography map application and began to lay out his plan. He needed to do this carefully. He considered bringing back a couple of his men to assist him with the old man's cabin surveillance. Roy knew that someone at that cabin would eventually lead him to his target. His thoughts kept going to Wells and wondered at the importance of these specific kids. It was a question that was beginning to monopolize his thoughts. When he passed the safe house, he recognized it was a trap just as he suspected. He had no proof yet, but he suspected Wells had tried to set him up.

As he was working, he spotted the message light from his custom security application. He had it programmed to monitor anything related to him or his team and relay it to him through secure encrypted channels. Roy had expected notifications, in fact, more notifications than what he had already received. This mission was already public. He knew that because the people who had escaped in the woods had gone to the police. It was on the news, but now there was more.

He saw his own face on one report. He opened it and read. The article indicated that he had led an assault on multiple official sites of federal buildings. The picture was old and not very clear, but he recognized his own eyes. As he checked deeper, he found a report indicating he and his team were marked as terrorists. He was not completely surprised. He had expected something like this from Wells, but two of the sites he was looking at were not sites or jobs he or his men were involved with. The most recent was the safe house he had checked out today. He then saw the picture of the witnesses. The witnesses were described as a highly trained assault team—a team of men he had never hired and would never have hired.

"Highly trained my ass," Roy said.

They all had indicated that they were working under his orders. He looked through a few more items and then began researching these men. His searches revealed enough for him to make an educated guess that Thompson hired these men.

Wells was behind this and had hired Thompson to take over the job and take him out. Unfortunately, they made the mistake of letting this leak out to the world press too soon. Wells was trying to preemptively cover his own ass.

Steve Roy sat and stared at the screen. He began to wonder more about this job and the targets he had been given. He re-opened his computer and began to research further the family he had been hired to eliminate. As he waited for his secure connections to be confirmed and encrypted, he thought about this job. He had never concerned himself with why the targets were to be apprehended or eliminated, only that he and his men were hired to do the job. They followed orders to capture or destroy the targets, steal documentation, spread misinformation, and complete other counter-intelligence missions—usually attacks in foreign countries where the US Armed forces could not go. They operated within the country a few times to eliminate a terrorist cell or sometimes to give a favored corporation an edge in contract negotiations. This job should have been the same, except this was something else.

His computer chimed when the connections were secure. He began searching to find out what he could about the target of this operation. He found public documentation linking the family with organized crime and even support of confirmed terrorist activity. All in all, it looked bad. There were staggering amounts of documented transactions and questionable purchases, but Roy was now suspicious. Nothing added up. No members of this family were terrorists. He had fought terrorists before. He dug further and then found traces of tampering within the documentation. Missing or mislabeled documents, sloppily edited files, and links that lead nowhere.

He changed his search and began searching in different paths, looking for information through other avenues. Soon, he came upon documentation of the trial. He found the pictures—these people were witnesses. This family of witnesses had taken down many influential people. They had been instrumental in bringing down organized political and corporate corruption.

Then he started researching the investigation. His connection had difficulty bypassing the security, and it took more time than he would have liked, but he was finally rewarded with the documentation he was after.

He studied the files looking for and finding items relating to himself. He had done tasks that were investigated concerning the case. While looking through the files, he found how those connections were researched and dismissed. He looked further and found references to several other men that he had worked with or for in the past. The investigations into some of these men, too, had been redirected. The investigations had been from inside. He kept searching and found what he had suspected to find at the root of it all.

Wells was there in the middle of the investigation. Roy studied Wells's contributions to the research. He had brought several people down, but there was more there. After reviewing several items, it became apparent to Roy that Wells had prevented several powerful people from being included in the suspect list from this investigation. The missions he and his team had taken from Wells had been instrumental in keeping these men from even being brought in for questioning. Some were even members of his own team that he had sent out on missions for the other people Wells had protected.

Roy sat back in his chair, his anger building, but he kept his focus. He stared at the screen, absorbing the magnitude of the situation. He and his team had been used and now were being set up. He began to trace the documentation back to the source. Who was pulling Wells's strings? It was hidden well.

He saw a name that gave him pause. He had used this man's connections to begin his current operation.

"Damn," he said, "if he's involved with Wells, this place is burned."

The man's company had been the broker in Roy acquiring this building off the records. He started planning to move his base operation to their backup location. He would need help. He had lost men on this job, and it was a job based on lies. Ordinarily, the deaths would not bother him. A job was a job. This job was different now. Wells was trying to eliminate him and his men.

In his mind, his plans were already changing when he heard a slight change in the sound of the AC unit. There was another sound as well; it was almost as if a voice was speaking, but from where he could not tell:

"Be ready, Buachaill."

He started from the voice and looked up from the screens, then he heard slight noises from the hall. He didn't have time to think about the voice.

As the door opened, he saw the reflection on the knob and saw the small disc fly into the room. He ducked to the right and covered his eyes with his arm as the flash of the small explosive went off. It was designed to blind him momentarily to give those entering the room an advantage, but he was better than they were. The five men who entered the room expected him to be at the desk, but he had kept moving and had his Smith & Wesson Stigma pistols drawn and ready. As the men paused a moment, surprised that he was not where they expected, he cut loose; seven shots in less than that many seconds. He subconsciously knew he had six shots remaining in his left gun and 7 in his right. He slipped the left-hand gun back in the holster and moved towards the door. He could hear others in the hallway. They were moving back preparing to storm the room.

He slid back between the file cabinets. He had kept himself

out of the sightline from the window. He reached behind himself and flipped the lever. The wall slid to the side silently as he slid back further and triggered the switch again. The wall slid shut again. Only then did he turn and run quietly along the concrete floor down between the insulated cinder block walls.

No sound could be heard on the other side of the wall. He had designed this building himself.

He followed two tunnels checking at each turn to ensure no one had entered his hidden routes. Finally, he came out in a storage room behind those in the hallway. He silently picked up two modified AR-15 rifles adapted to be fully automatic. He checked the ammo loads, then ensured he had extra magazines for his pistols and the AR-15s. He then reloaded the magazines for his pistols; ten rounds for each gun and an additional magazine for each.

He then turned back and grabbed his newest weapon. It was a new technology that was little known to the public. A personal directional electronic pulse gun referred to as a PDEP. He verified it was fully charged by viewing the lights on the battery and grabbed the extra battery pack to be sure. He had not tested this weapon in live-fire yet. This would be a good a time as any.

He listened to the men outside. They had lost him but knew he had not left the building. He arranged several claymore mines around the room. They were searching intently, and he knew they would eventually get to this room. He ran the trip wires around the room, careful not to make noise. He went back into the wall and slipped inside again, leaving the door open. He moved back a few steps to where he knew there was an extra wall between him and the storeroom. Then he heard them enter the place. He pushed the button, and the door started to slide closed. The men searching saw and called out:

"We got him!"

They stormed into the room, trying to reach the sliding door before it closed. All of them were in the room when the door tripped the claymores. They didn't stand a chance.

He knew who sent them. He now knew he had to become a ghost.

The room was a mass of debris and bodies. When he looked back in, he could not tell how many were there. At least six, he thought. The others would not know for sure if he was among them. He set the timer for the building defenses and left down the tunnel leading under the parking lot to the back of the basement of the dry cleaner. He listened, and when he was sure no one was there, he slipped out and was gone. Moments after the door closed, his office building collapsed—the entire storefront falling back into the hole. Now it would be some time before anyone would be able to tell who had been there when it collapsed. He wished he could have grabbed more weapons. He was glad he had sent his men away earlier. He knew they could handle themselves. They would not be caught.

35

Pursuit

Two blocks away from the safehouse, Thompson was working very hard to keep his anger in check.

"Pull over here," he said. The driver signaled and pulled the big SUV into a small parking lot. The second SUV that was traveling with them pulled into the next space and waited for Thompson's orders.

The men at the site had kept him informed the whole time, right up to the building collapsing. They said no one could have survived it and they bugged out before he and his men could arrive. Thompson had planned on eliminating both infiltration teams as well as all the support crew in the vans. No loose ends was his plan. Thompson knew that plan was now lost. He had not expected Roy to destroy his own building. That surprised him, but he knew Roy would not have been caught in that building as it came down. Roy had to have a way out. Thompson now had to reevaluate his plans. Even though he couldn't eliminate the other men, he still had to get Roy. He had to think; he couldn't just guess where Roy would come out. He had to outsmart him and cut him off. He thought about the surrounding area as he checked his maps and the roadways; he made his choice. Roy would not take the quickest route away; that would be too obvious. He directed his men to turn around. They headed back a few blocks to where there would be more traffic for Roy to try to hide. Thompson had to convince himself he made the right choice.

Steve Roy climbed into his old truck and made sure all the vans were gone. He picked the old '63 F100 since it had no GPS or electronics to track him by. When he was satisfied no one was left, he pulled out in the opposite direction and drove. He was watching for pursuit for two blocks—not able to believe he was away clean. Just when he was about to relax, two SUVs pulled out behind him. He was sure they were after him with the blacked-out windows and what Roy recognized as fake municipality plates. He led them out of town and onto an old highway where fewer cars were there to contend with. They sped along at breakneck speed.

Roy had automatically turned on his jammer so they could not send a signal to call for backup. As he was weaving through the traffic, he allowed the two SUVs to close in on him. The first one pulled alongside the passenger side of his truck. The window on the SUV rolled down, and Thompson was staring at him from the far side. Thompson kept his driver between Roy and himself. The driver was about to ram Roy into the center barrier when Roy lifted the PDEP and fired it at the front of the SUV. When he pulled the trigger, the electronics in the SUV went out immediately, and the engine died.

The SUV lost speed and rolled to a stop with smoke rolling from the engine compartment. Thompson knew it would never run again. All their radios and phones were burning hot, their batteries letting out trailing smoke. The man driving was wearing an earpiece and had instant third-degree burns in his ear.

Thompsons' phone burned through his breast pocket. As he struggled to extract his phone from his shirt, the radio on his shoulder melted into his arm. He cursed as he threw it to the floor, burning his hand in the process.

The cabin filled with the acrid smell of burning electronics. Thompson was out of the vehicle and moving fast to get away from the wreckage. A civilian car had stalled in the far lane—it had also been affected by the pulse. Thompson left his men to contend with the SUV and approached the vehicle. That car was not burning, and Thompson needed it. The owner was able to restart the car. It was running rough, but the driver pulled away and escaped the approaching mercenary. Thompson would need to find another way to escape.

Roy sped away and flipped the trigger with one hand to release the battery from the PDEP. It dropped onto his center console directly into a coffee cup holder. It was so hot it started to melt the plastic. He then clicked in the second battery that was clipped to his belt.

The second SUV was gaining on him. They would have no idea what had happened to their associates. They began closing on Roy.

They rammed the back trying to run Roy off the road. Suddenly as they were moving in for a second ram, Roy spun the wheel and pulled the emergency brake. The truck spun around, coming dangerously close to rolling over. Roy slammed it into reverse, released the emergency brake, and jammed the peddle to the floor. He stuck his PDEP through the window and angled it back at the pursuing car while driving in reverse. When he pulled the trigger, their engine stopped instantly, and all the electronics in the vehicle started to burn. The first pulse he fired had blown the limiter circuit on the gun. The directional coil melted itself as it fired a pulse much stronger than the first. The SUV burst into flames as all electronic wires shorted at the same time. The men in the second SUV struggled to remove the cables from their radios and phones as they melted into their skin. The two cars behind the SUV died and coasted to a stop.

Roy spun the truck back around and the burning weapon behind him into the bed. He sped on and left the highway, disappearing into the suburbs. His thoughts were no longer on hunting the old man and the kids. Now his thoughts turned to killing Thompson and most likely Wells. He had been double-crossed twice on this deal.

They would both pay. But first, he had to go back to the old man's cabin and watch.

36

Caleb and Frank

Caleb and Frank worked out the details of the plan together. Frank had provided Caleb with the information he had brought with him of past missions in which Steve Roy had been engaged. Caleb worked out a plan to draw the Mercenary and his team close. He would funnel them through the trees, making them think they were coming in unobserved. It would leave them exposed to the most accessible line of fire from the cabin and keep them away from the hidden path they would use for escape. They hoped to take out as many as possible along the way to reduce the number of men coming after them.

Caleb observed the tactics that Steve Roy used in many missions. "He and his men won't fall for all of the traps I set, but if I set some that are easy to find and trip, we may get them to be overconfident and get ahead of their thinkin'."

"I think he may be smarter than this; from what I have been told, he should have been able to complete this mission easily and without having this much trouble," said Frank.

Caleb looked again at the documentation. "I reckon you are right about that, but he may have brought in some men on this that are less skilled. Maybe there's something else at play here, it's hard to tell at this moment, but we should be prepared for anything."

"It could be," said Frank, "the reports I read indicated that he sent his regular team away."

"Either way, I have to go set up some more surprises for our guests. You know what to set up in here." He then took the bag with him and stepped out the back into the woods. Frank grabbed the second bag and began setting up the cabin. They knew that someone would be coming for them, and they wanted to be ready. He set up the ammo packs lining them up so they would be prepared. Frank did not like the thought of using Tom as bait, but he could find no other way to ensure that they could draw the mercenaries into the trap. They worked for a full day and would be ready to get Tom in the morning.

37

Annie

Annie woke up and realized immediately that Sarah was not in her bed. Panic ran through her.

She got up and went to Tom's room. She saw them on the bed looking like they had fallen asleep while in the middle of an intimate conversation. Sarah was curled around Tom, her head on his chest. As she looked at them, she saw a shimmer near Sarah, a sort of distortion in the air.

In a sudden flash, a vision overcame Annie as she looked at her sleeping friend. She could see Sarah looking for Tom, but with every moment spent searching for him she was being drawn farther away, her calls growing softer in the distance of the waking dream.

Annie's eyes cleared, and she was back in the room once more. She was unsure what to do, but she knew it would not happen if they remained by their side. She jotted down a note and left it where she suspected Tom would see it.

After leaving the note, Annie went out to help the Chief saddle the horses. She didn't tell the man about her vision, though she had no reason to keep it secret.

After the horses were ready, she and the Chief rode farther out than she had ever gone from the cabin. He instructed her to listen to the animals and birds as they rode and interpret the messages they were passing to each other. He told her to take note of the plant life as they passed. He questioned her from time to time about what she had seen and heard on this ride. He praised her responses about plants and sounds and the secret language of the wilderness. She pointed out when she noticed changes.

Annie grew more aware of other sounds just on the edge of her understanding; voices that she felt more than heard seemed to be trying to tell her something important if she could only understand what it was.

Bits of these feelings had come over her in the previous days, and she had brought them up to the chief. He had then told her of the woman they would see that day.

The Chief warned her not to speak to this woman unless she was first asked a question. He also told her not to lie.

Soon they arrived at a small house in the woods. The sounds of the forest had died away gradually as they approached. The only sound here was the occasional cricket chirp and a bird calling in the distance.

The Chief smiled at Annie and with a gesture indicated she should remain where she was. The Chief dismounted, handed her the reins, and then approached the door. It opened before he reached the porch. A woman stepped out into the sunlight and smiled at the Chief. She appeared at first glance to be about the same age as the Chief but when she turned to look past the Chief Annie saw a face much younger—closer to her mother's age. The memory of her mother brought a tear to her eye. She had not thought of her for several days, but now those emotions came crowding back.

The sadness on Annie's face was apparent to the woman—the smile she had worn for the Chief faded when she saw Annie. She looked back to the Chief with the question in her eyes, even before she spoke.

"This is the one of whom you spoke when you contacted me?"

The Chief nodded and waited. The woman looked back at Annie, slowly shook her head, and turned back to her cabin. A warm wind had come up from nowhere as the woman froze in place. The grass in the clearing swayed back and forth, but the trees were still.

Suddenly a flock of sparrows burst up from the forest, encircling the woman and the Chief, singing in voices almost human. The sparrows left the two elders and circled Annie three times before flying up and over the trees.

For a brief moment, Annie felt she could understand their song, and the painful memory of her mother was gone; for that moment she was filled with joy. Suddenly the wind and the birds were gone, and silence returned to the clearing. The woman said something Annie could not understand, but when the Chief answered, Annie heard him mention the name of Lady Maribel.

The mysterious woman looked back at Annie again and reluctantly nodded. She stepped back into her house and momentarily later stepped out carrying a soft blanket. She closed the heavy door behind her. When the door was locked she turned and whistled.

An old donkey stepped around from the back side of the house. The woman placed the blanket over its back and mounted it easily. She rode next to the Chief as he walked back to the horses. He introduced Annie to the woman but did not say her name. The woman nodded at Annie, her eyes lingering on her necklace and pendant. Annie returned the nod silently and respectfully.

"Annie," said the woman. "Did the birds tell you my name?"

Annie looked at her a moment and then the feeling she received while the birds circled her came back; then she nodded. "You are Sunshine."

The woman smiled as she too nodded. "Yes, I am Sunshine."

She then turned and looked at the Chief as he mounted. "Wait a moment," she said, then turned and whistled again. A small horse came trotting through the trees and came up to Sunshine. She took the lead that was hanging from the harness and handed it to the Chief.

"We will need her," she said simply. "Let's go."

They followed the Chief as they left on their return trip. Along the way, the Chief again instructed Annie to listen, observe and be ready to answer when questioned. The woman rode beside her and silently studied the girl.

"Child, what was the vision you had this morning?" Sunshine asked.

Annie meant to ask how the woman knew of that but decided better of it. Instead, she turned to her and relayed the color, the feelings, and the diminishing sound of Sarah's call. The woman nodded and turned to the Chief. "We must not delay. We must be back there today."

The Chief flicked his reins, urging his horse to move faster.

38

Sarah and Tom

Tom woke up at the cabin with Sarah lying next to him. She had one arm draped over his chest and her soft breath was moving her hair that was partially covering her face. He reached over, gently pushed her hair back, and gazed at her face. Then very carefully moved off the bed and quietly stepped into the bathroom. He was completely smitten by her. As she slept, he cleaned up and dressed. He had decided that he would return to Caleb's cabin today. He had to find Caleb and Frank and find out what was going on. The waiting and not knowing what they would need to do next was getting to him. He had thought he would be more involved after going with Frank and Caleb to get the evidence files, but he felt he had been pushed back. He understood why but could not shake his nature. He had to be doing something, to be more involved. He felt he could make it there unseen and find out what he needed to do to keep Sarah and Annie safe. He knew Caleb and the Chief would not be there forever. Frank was not going to be an agent anymore if he kept working outside the official parameters like he was on this case. Tom was beginning to feel the responsibility for their safety and just needed to have more information so he could keep the girls safe. He quietly stepped into the kitchen and grabbed a couple of leftover rolls from the previous night's dinner. Next to the rolls was the note from Annie.

Tom,

Chief and I have gone to find another friend to help us. We will be back tonight before supper. I can tell you want to go find Caleb and Frank. I think you were planning to sneak away today. Please don't go anywhere, it doesn't feel right for you to leave Sarah behind now. I think Caleb and Frank will be back for you soon, so don't look for them. I get the feeling it would be a bad idea, especially today. Please stay with Sarah, something is not feeling right. I can't explain. Stay near her today. I just feel like someone is coming for her. Don't tell her yet, wait for me. I don't know why but don't tell her. You keep her safe today, don't leave her alone. Please!

Annie

Tom read the note again. He had not yet decided to go until he had awoken that morning. He was impressed that Annie had been able to tell. He would stay today—he didn't like the thought of anyone coming for Sarah. He turned back toward the living room and was startled to see Sarah standing there. She had pulled on a shirt and was looking at him.

"Where are you going?" she asked.

"Nowhere today," he said, "shall I make us some breakfast?"

Sarah laughed, "You'll make breakfast for me? I would love that." She then sat at the table watching him as he prepared the food. He wasn't the neatest cook and was making a mess, but she could tell he knew what he was doing with this dish.

She knew she felt more for Tom than anyone she had dated before. She would not let herself admit it was more than she was ready to accept.

She watched him from start to finish and then they enjoyed their breakfast together. When they heard a horse approaching, Sarah jumped up, ran back to Tom's room, grabbed her clothes, and disappeared into the bathroom. Tom laughed a little as she ran. He had already dressed himself enough to be decent.

Caleb and Frank walked in the door. "Did you make enough for us too?" Frank said as he noticed the aroma of the breakfast.

"I can make more," Tom answered as he stood up from the table to get started.

Caleb looked at him when the shower started in the bathroom. "You will have to protect that girl's love. A gift like that when given can't be wasted."

"I know," Tom said. He handed Caleb the note from Annie.

Caleb read the note and quietly handed it to Frank. "I was going to take Tom back with us to my cabin. I was thinking that he has to be seen there to set our trap. I saw something on the way here—someone had been watching the place." Frank started, but Caleb continued, "our trap will work, but now I think we have to decide if we are staying here till the Chief gets back or if we are taking both of them with us."

Frank tucked the note into his pocket as Sarah stepped out of the bathroom ready for the day. She came over and greeted them while gently scolding them for being away too long.

"Frank, I am so glad you are here. Can you tell me if you have heard anything from my family yet?" She was staring into Frank's eyes with worry.

"They are fine," said Frank, "your father is upset that we haven't returned you to them right away. He was threatening lawsuits till he saw the security team we have assigned to your family. He then listened while we explained the situation. He still wants us to return you so he can take your whole family out of state. We informed him we can't transport you to them safely yet, but I assured him that you would be returned to them soon."

"He won't be able to protect them if I am there," she looked at Tom, "and if I go home, he will never let me see Tom or Annie again." She thought for a moment. "I'm staying here with you." The look in her eyes would broach no argument.

Caleb gave a slight smile, nodded to Tom, and walked out the back door. "Come with me, Tom." Tom grabbed his shoes and a jacket by the door and followed. He and Caleb took care of the horse and cleaned the stalls in the shed to prepare a place for the Chief and Annie's return so they could quickly bed down their horses. Tom worked silently as Caleb described his plan. It would put Tom in danger, but he would have to be seen at the other cabin at least once. They would draw in whoever was stalking them and either capture them if possible or—if need be—eliminate them. Tom had thought before that he wouldn't be able to kill anyone, but with the threat to Sarah, he knew he would do what he had to. They finished their tasks and as they were heading back to the cabin.

After they had arrived, Caleb spoke in a low whisper:

"There was a flash of light from the forest as we made our way; we are being watched—"

Tom interrupted him, "Annie and the Chief are coming back here. How will we warn them?"

Caleb looked at him, "The Chief will know long before they get here. I will leave word for him that only he will be able to read. Sarah, get ready to go. We are heading back to my cabin."

39

Steve Roy

Steve Roy had seen the flash of light as well. He had followed the old man and Frank since leaving the cabin. He kept his distance and tracked them very carefully. He immediately realized that someone else was following them, shadowing their movements. It didn't take any great leap to realize this was likely another of Thompson's mercenaries.

This one had more talent than the rest but was still making mistakes that allowed Steve to avoid his detection. He kept close enough to find a place to observe this new cabin where they were staying. He crept around slowly, his camouflage keeping him hidden. He stalked the other mercenary till he had a clear shot. He waited for Thompson's man to set up. Steve scoped the distance and wind. He sighted the man and waited. When Caleb came out of the cabin, Steve didn't turn his head; he kept his eyes on the man. This man was prepared like a sniper but did not have a rifle. Instead, he had a camera.

Steve watched the man's finger move, depressing the shutter as he took several pictures of the cabin. Steve recognized him. He knew the man as Scott; he never knew his first name. They had never worked together before, though Roy had considered bringing him along on a few missions.

When Frank and the kids went out the other side, Scott was unable to capture them on camera. The cabin blocked his line of sight. He started to move, but Caleb had caught sight of him. The twang of the bowstring sounded then the arrow pierced the camera knocking it from Scott's hand. The arrow would have been through his eye if he hadn't moved at that moment. Scott left the useless camera and backed out into the cover of the trees as quickly as possible. Steve Roy could hear his noisy retreat.

Steve remained still and did not reveal his own location. He watched Caleb carefully. He was impressed with the speed with which the bow had been raised and fired. He remembered the sound of the arrow flying past his own head and knew that the cameraman would not be returning without backup.

It was an unnerving sound, so close to death.

He watched Caleb walk over and retrieve his arrow. He took the camera with him and turned away. Steve smiled slightly as he watched the scene. He knew he could have taken out the old man this time. He proved himself in his own eyes again. There was a whisper of wind in his ear, almost a voice.

"Maybe, Buachaill, if we be lettin' you." This time, the voice didn't startle him; he just accepted it and backed out slowly and silently. He had to stay back and observe from a distance.

40

Thompson

"What do you mean, an arrow?" Thompson didn't believe what he was hearing.

He had discovered the cabin from the report Steve Roy had submitted. He dispatched Scott, who he thought was his best recon man, to observe and report back if the kids were there.

He could say that he might have seen the boy, but he didn't get the pictures. An arrow had destroyed his camera, so there was no real evidence he could submit to implicate Johnston as complicit in the kids' disappearance. Wells had engaged Thompson on a plan to discredit both Frank Johnston and Ward Jamison. Thompson had promised results; he would not report this setback.

Scott repeated the same story. He had found the cabin and followed Johnston and some old man on horses deeper into the woods to a second cabin. There, he was trying to get photographic evidence when he thought he saw the boy. When he tried to get into position to take a picture, the old man was in the way—no clear shot. Scott had tried to move to get a picture of the people coming out of the cabin on the other side when the arrow pierced his camera inches from his face. He bugged out; he didn't even bring his camera back with him. He did say he could lead them back to the new cabin. Thompson started making new plans. He would have to be there himself this time. He couldn't afford any more mistakes. He was working on getting all the jobs that Roy usually booked. If he was unable to catch a few kids, he would never get those assignments.

"Get the guys ready. We are going back to that fucking old man's cabin today," said Thompson.

Scott nodded and stepped back out to get the team ready. He was already on Thompson's shit list and was ready to get back onto his good side as quickly as possible. Thompson had a reputation for how he dealt with team members that disappointed him.

Within 20 minutes Thompson and his best team were suited up and rolling in new trucks. All ten of them were dressed for fighting in the woods. Wells had been pissed about having to clean up the mess on the highway but had been able to get a press release explaining the car chase as federal agents going after a known terrorist. The SUVs had to be towed out of there before anything could be inspected by local police. Wells was still working to smooth that over. Thompson was not going to bother him about details of what happened. His men were still wearing the bandages from the burns when their radios and headsets burst into flames, but they were all ready to go. They wanted this just as bad as Thompson.

Thompson was hoping that Roy would be there too. In fact, he wanted to take that one out himself.

41

Sunshine

Frank brought Sarah and Tom back into the Chief's cabin after Caleb called them back. They would wait for the Chief and then return to Caleb's cabin. He knew that area better and had already set up the perimeter. He would have the Chief take the kids to a new place. This one was compromised. He would go out today to make sure they were not followed again. Frank would have to help him. The Chief would be needed to get the kids to safety.

"No," said Tom, "I am not being left behind again. I can handle it. I can't stand being left here wondering what's going on."

Caleb knew how Tom was feeling, but he couldn't risk it. He had to keep them safe. They were all his responsibility now. He would not take that chance, but he thought he knew what would get him to come back.

"Tom, I can't have you stay with us. I have set the traps; I will be moving fast, and I need to know you are all safe so I can do what I need to do." Caleb turned and looked out at the path leading to the roadway. "I will need you to come straight back here to keep the girls safe. Work with the Chief directly and get them moving as soon as you can."

Tom finally relented; he could see that Sarah was scared now. The man showing up had broken the sense of calm that had reached her at the Chief's cabin. She now knew they were not as safe as it had seemed. Tom would do whatever he could to get her back to where she could feel safe again. She was more important to him now than his desire to help stop these men from coming after them.

They heard the horses before they saw them. The Chief led the small group into the corral and dismounted. He noted the stalls were set up and ready. He also noted Gray was there. It would be good to introduce Caleb to the woman; his smile faded when he turned back to her. The look on her face was one of intense concentration. She was impatient to proceed. There was danger here, and she could feel it. They quickly put up the horses and the donkey. Annie wanted to do more, but the woman was impatient and urged them to move quickly. Annie grained the horses and the donkey. She also gave Gray a greeting, grained him, and gave him a treat of an apple she had grabbed from the tree as they passed. They moved into the cabin to find everyone there. The woman didn't wait for introductions. She walked right up to Caleb and reached out to touch him. Satisfied he was real, she took his hand in her own. After several seconds she spoke.

"Chosen, your charge is important. You must protect them; they are the future. Therefore, they must survive at all costs even to your staying past your allotted time."

She then turned to Frank and took his hand. "You are coming to a change. You will no longer remain as you are but must become more. If you do not succeed, the Chosen will not succeed."

She turned back to the Chief, "Grandfather, you did not say how important this is. If you had, I would not have hesitated."

The Chief gave a slight smile, "Sunshine, would you have believed me?"

"No, probably not, but I would have listened," Sunshine said.

Annie looked at the Chief; she could not believe the woman was his Granddaughter. He did not look old enough to be this woman's grandfather. He introduced her first to Caleb and then to the others.

"Sunshine, this is Caleb Teach; he is the Chosen I taught you of so many years ago. Caleb, this is Sunshine, my son's first daughter. She is going to help me teach Annie." Sunshine gazed into Caleb's eyes. Annie recognized the moment when Sunshine had her vision. Sunshine did not say what she saw, just turned as the Chief continued the introductions to Frank, then Tom, and Sarah.

Sunshine said to Frank. "Stay with the Chosen. He will need you very soon."

"Tom, you have a great responsibility. You must protect Sarah and Annie. You will make mistakes, but you have great potential." She turned to the Chief. "He will need you as well, Grandfather, as much as you needed a son."

Sarah was watching Sunshine; something about her drew Sarah in. "Sunshine, do I know you? Have we met?"

Sunshine looked at her, "Child, we have met. You were with a group that was providing aid to my family during the drought. You were there out of kindness, not as the others who were there out of requirement. Your kindness is remembered. Perhaps now I can pay you back."

When she turned to Annie, she spoke, "Annie, forgive my

hesitation and silence earlier. I have watched you on the way back. You are now my novice, my ward. I will be your guide and will be responsible for you. I feel you can exceed my teaching, and I will become your student before we end our relationship. Sarah, you also will need to learn. You will join us, please." Sarah nodded; she was in awe.

Sunshine then turned back to Caleb and Frank. "You have plans. Go over them with Grandfather and Tom. They both will have roles to play soon. Unfortunately, I cannot see them. But the trouble is coming. Send Tom back to us before it starts. We will need him."

Sunshine then took the girls, and they went to the other room to begin.

Caleb spoke to the Chief. "Your granddaughter is quite a woman."

The Chief nodded and smiled. "She is that." The men then sat around the table and began discussing plans. They were out the door in less than 15 minutes and on the way back to Caleb's cabin.

After they left, Sunshine prepared the girls for what was coming. She arranged a hiding place for Sarah in the back room away from the windows between the fireplace and the large built-in cabinet. "When I tell you to, you will hide here." She handed Sarah the shotgun that had been leaning on the wall in the other room. "Keep this here so you can get to it when you are here. Brace this against the wall and pull the trigger if someone you do not know comes for you. Only come out if one of us calls you." Sarah nodded as Sunshine moved the cart with firewood in front of her hiding place to protect her further. "Now for you," Sunshine said as she took Annie and fit her in the space between the refrigerator and the cast iron stove. She gave Annie a 22 handgun, "I know you know how to use this; make sure it is within your reach when you are here. You aim true and trust your instincts." Annie nodded and calmed herself as Sunshine moved the table to make someone coming into the kitchen walk around to the far end so Annie would have more time to see the intruder before they saw her. Sunshine then pulled the chair in front of Annie's space to provide more cover. Sunshine looked over both hiding places. She wished she had more time but knew it would not be enough. She stepped to the front door and sat on the bench next to the door. The danger was coming; she would be ready. She spoke with the girls to keep them calm. When the birds let them know it was time, she would put the girls in their places.

Caleb had led the men on foot down a different path back to his cabin. They arrived back at the cabin, coming in from the opposite side of the clearing down a well-hidden path. After they arrived at the cabin, Frank took Tom around the front, and they went inside. Caleb and the Chief made sure their escape route was clear and the ATV was still hidden along the protected path, then returned to the cabin.

"Are you sure he was seen?" Caleb asked.

"Yes," said the Chief, "The man watching from the ridge saw him here. They will come for him."

"Tom," said Caleb, "you know this was the plan just to draw them in. I know you want to stay, but I can't let you."

"I know." Tom hesitated for a moment, then continued, "I have to get back to the girls. I wish I could do more to help you here."

Caleb nodded then turned back to the window to watch.

Frank gave Tom instructions to get back through the woods

to the Chief's cabin. The Chief would take him past the traps set by Caleb earlier. Then Tom would have the ATV that Frank had left at the site. This would get Tom back to the cabin quickly. He would have to follow the path as instructed or be seen. The Chief would return and would be helping Caleb and Frank with the mercenary team they expected. Caleb lit the fireplace and started putting some green wood on the fire to increase the smoke. This would draw attention to the cabin and hopefully draw in the mercenaries.

Tom was torn. He didn't want to go back. He wanted to stay and fight with them, but the Chief said he would be needed to help the girls. This convinced him, and he agreed. They left, going out the hidden passage through the back shed into the woods. They arrived at the ATV with no issues. The Chief said his goodbye and melted back into the woods. Tom pushed the button to engage the batteries on the ATV; it was an electric motor. He had read about them but didn't know they were in production. It would be relatively quiet, and he should be able to make it without being noticed. He reluctantly began following the hidden trail back up to the Chief's cabin.

The Chief quickly arrived back at Caleb's cabin and joined Frank and Caleb as they prepared for the inevitable. It was not long before the first sounds came from the woods. The sounds of the branches being whipped up as if by a flock of birds. The first traps that Caleb had set released the birds to fly up. The man overlooked the tripping mechanism. It appeared to him that he had just disturbed the birds. They were as good as any warning flare to Caleb and the Chief. It was the Chief who saw them first; they were on alert. The Chief slid out through the same hidden path. He was a better fighter out in the woods. Frank and Caleb would defend the cabin. It had to be convincing to keep the attacker's attention on this cabin and not go after the girls. The next sound was that of a man crying out as a branch whipped out, stinging nettles striking his face. He didn't notice the cut on his leg over the pain in his face. He poured water on his face to relieve the burning.

He spotted the blood on his leg. It was spurting too fast; the trap had opened an artery. By the time he realized he was in trouble, it was too late. He slumped over and died with no more sound.

His partners spread out and approached from different directions; they never knew their man was dead. The next trap was less successful. This man saw the tripping mechanism and sprung it by throwing a stone.

The others were moving cautiously now. The birds and the cry earlier had them on edge. As they moved in, they tripped more noisemakers.

One man met up with a snake, lucky that his boots were thick leather and above his calf. The bite did not get through to his skin. He tried to kill the snake with his knife, but it got away. At this time, his luck ran out; he turned back towards the cabin and took two steps when a branch sprung around, driving the spike into his arm. He yelled out and backed off the point, causing more damage in his panic. He wrapped his arm with his bandana, trying to stop the bleeding as he stepped under the branch, cursing to himself. He was in range now and could see the cabin but would have to be careful with his arm. He aimed and waited for the signal. They were covering all sides except towards the clearing where they planned to trap them. The other mercenaries were luckier and were in a better position. They opened fire on the cabin, knowing they would not penetrate the logs but trying to drive the men out and capture the boy. They knew he was with them as they had been watching as they came in but unaware of the hidden path away from the cabin, they had missed him leaving. As they were shooting, the Chief rose behind the man adjusting the wrap on his arm to stop the bleeding. He never knew the Chief was there until the blade entered his back, severing the spinal cord. He died instantly. The other mercenaries continued shooting, but gunfire was returning to them from the cabin; it was more accurate than expected. Caleb had quickly risen above the window sill and fired three shots through the face of the man shooting in from that side. Now only five men were left attacking the cabin.

Thompson had kept Scott with him when he sent the team to attack the old man's cabin. He and Scott went up the path back towards the other house where the man had lost his camera. Thompson didn't want to miss an opportunity to catch someone there. He trusted his team to clear that cabin and follow along, effectively keeping himself out of the fight again. He would take the glory when they succeeded, but he covered his own ass as effectively as anyone.

42

Caught

Tom stopped when he heard the gunfire. He knew he had to continue, but he couldn't bear the thought of losing Caleb, the Chief, and Frank. So, after a moment, he turned back. He stopped further out than he had been when he first got on the ATV. He crept in towards the cabin, trying to see what was happening. Even as the gunfire got sparser, he was more anxious; he began moving quicker towards the cabin. Suddenly, the bush beside him erupted, and a hand clamped over his mouth. He was pulled back and forced to the ground. The weight of the man on his back held him down as he struggled, till the man whispered in his ear. "Stop it, kid. You almost walked right onto one of the old man's traps."

Tom didn't recognize the voice, but whoever it was had indeed stopped him from getting hung up on a hazardous trap. As he looked, he saw the tripping mechanism just before he stepped into it. The man on his back tossed a rock at it. The branches swung around with sharpened spikes at eye level.

"Don't move, kid." The man kept a knee on Tom's back and rose. He brought a rifle up to his shoulder and squeezed off a couple of shots. There was less shooting now; the shots were few and far between.

"There, that should make it more even now. I am sure your friends can handle what's left." The man looked down at Tom. "Now, let's get out of here."

The man pulled Tom to his feet and nearly dragged him back to the ATV.

"Kid, I saw you heading out… Now I think we better get to where you were going. Someone worse than me is heading up there on the main path now."

Tom didn't know if he could trust this man, but he had little choice. He had no weapon handy, and this man had several available. So they got back on the ATV, and Tom drove them on. His thoughts were flying from Caleb, Frank, and the Chief, to the girls. He had to figure out how to protect them—he had to.

"Kid, you have been hard to find. I know you have no reason to trust me, but I am not here to kill you. I was sent to get you alive. I'm Steve Roy"

Tom slowed down, "You killed my family and were going to kill Annie! Why the fuck should I take you back to her?"

Roy just shrugged and said, "The ass-hat that hired me has altered my deal too many times. I don't think I want to work for him anymore. He sent someone else after you; now he is after the girls. Let's see if we can't get there before that other jerk."

Tom gunned it. They sped through the woods almost too fast for the path. He nearly tipped on a couple of turns, but they arrived soon enough. The truck was there on the track blocking the entrance to the clearing. Tom was upset and started to rush forward. The man behind him grabbed his arm to stop him, then said, "Kid, we may be late to this party, but we are smarter than those two. Follow my lead, and don't say anything till I speak." He still held Tom by the arm and now had his gun pointed at him. "Just for show, kid," he said. Tom didn't feel reassured.

Thompson and his man were next to the door waiting. They knew they had found the girls but were unsure if they were alone. The hesitation allowed Sunshine to check Sarah in the back room. She checked Annie again, and now sure that neither could be seen from outside, she opened the door.

Thompson had his gun up and ordered her to step out. He held the gun on her as she stepped out onto the porch. Thompson barked his order to Scott. "Go in there and get the girls."

The man turned to go into the house. Thompson held the gun on Sunshine and was taunting her; she just defiantly stared at him. Then Steve Roy appeared, pulling the boy along with him.

"Well, Thompson, I would have never expected you to be able to find them here," said Roy, "you must have hired someone smarter to do it for you."

"Roy, you are an asshole. You always were," said Thompson, "Thanks for bringing me the boy, though. That will go a long way to making me tops on Wells' list. Unfortunately, you're not going to get the primo jobs anymore."

"Neither are you, ya dumb bastard. You fucked up so many times that Wells is probably setting you up to take the fall for all this crap."

Thompson paused for a moment, thinking. It sounded like Wells, but he would be free and clear if he brought in the kids.

"No, I will have the kids here, and Wells will reward me for closing this out. Johnston is going down for this along with you," Thompson said.

Roy laughed. "You believe that, and you're going to be real disappointed. I can't believe you're this clueless. I knew you couldn't be trusted, but dang, I didn't know you were this stupid too."

Thompson turned away from the woman. The instant his gun was pointed away from her, Roy turned and fired. His shot took Thompson by surprise. His gun went flying away. His hand was numb and worthless, stinging with shock. He ducked back behind his truck. Tom was running the moment the shots started. "Fuck kid, get back here!" said Roy as he was forced to chase after him. He couldn't afford to lose the kid now. Tom was at the back door of the cabin and through the door in a flash. Thompson's man inside the cabin had heard the shots outside and was about to burst out the front when Tom burst through the back door. As the man turned towards this noise, his gun struck the cabinet throwing off his aim. His shot went wide and through the rear door frame causing Roy to dive to the side. Tom had ducked behind the table. He reached for the shotgun that was always by the fireplace, but it wasn't there. He turned back to see the man coming around the table. He turned his weapon on Tom. "Hey, dumbass, I am supposed to take you kids alive. What the fuck you thinking of jumping out like that? Now get up here and come over by the front door. Who was out there shooting at the boss?"

Tom just stared at the gun pointed at him. "He said his name was Steve."

"Fuck." said the Mercenary.

They heard the truck tearing away in a cloud of dust. The man looked up out the front window, "What the hell, where's he going?"

Roy padded in through the back door behind the man. He brought his gun up and pressed the barrel against the man's neck. "You might just want to put that down now." The man dropped his weapon on the table and put his hands on his head.

"Hi Roy," he said. "Been a while."

"Yeah, Scott, it has. It looks like Thompson bugged out on you. I warned you about him years ago, didn't I?"

"Yeah, but a guy's gotta work."

Roy said, "Well yeah but working for Thompson will get you killed; now sit your ass down. Kid get something to strap this guy down with."

Tom got up, grabbed one of the horse ropes, and tied the man up to the chair, legs and arms both, as well as around his waist.

"So, what's the deal with Wells?" Roy asked.

"He didn't like you backing out on him," said Scott. "He is pinning a bunch of crap on you; enough of it's true, so you're pretty much screwed."

"Yeah, that much I already knew. What I mean is, why does he want these kids so bad."

Scott looked at him. "I really don't know. Didn't concern me too much."

"Where's Sunshine?" Annie asked as she stepped out of her hiding place.

"I am here, child." Sunshine was walking in the back door; she had Thompson's weapon. "Sarah, come now. We have to go."

Sarah stepped out of the room where Sunshine had hidden her carrying the shotgun. Tom stepped over and wrapped

Sarah in a hug and then pulled Annie in as well. "I thought I was too late."

Sunshine stepped over and again said, "We have to go now." She turned to Roy and said, "Sir, thank you for helping us. Now you have to go find the man that you let escape. He will be back for us again and you."

43

Thompson vs. Roy

The firefight was slowing down. The men attacking the cabin had noticed that the sound of shooting at the cabin was diminishing, but shots coming from within the building were not. Two of the remaining men slipped up to the side door of the cabin.

One took a glance into the window next to the door. Caleb had just emptied his Remington pistols out the window opposite of these men. He signaled his partner to open the door. They had the drop on the old man. The door opened silently, and the man started to slip in with his weapon trained on Caleb's back. Frank looked over at Caleb, watching him load his guns. He caught the movement in the corner of his eye and turned and fired three quick shots. The man fell back out the door dead before his ass hit the ground. The other man bugged out back towards the trees. Caleb calmly turned, fired a single shot through the closing door, and caught the man between the shoulder blades just as he arrived at the tree line; he fell forward and dragged himself behind the first tree. He was dead moments later.

Frank moved to the side door, pushed the dead man outside, and closed the door again. When he turned back, Caleb was looking at him.

"Thanks for covering my back," said Caleb, "Sunshine said I would need you. I guess she was right."

Frank nodded and went back to his post.

There were two men left in the woods. Their associates were not answering their radios. They decided to bug out and retreated, covering for each other till they could turn and run. As they were moving out, they came across some of their associates. They were unnerved at each one they found and were sprinting by the time they reached the edge of the woods. They burst from the trees right in front of the truck barreling down the mountain. Thompson didn't slow as he plowed into them. He didn't stop after; he just kept going. 'Needed a new team anyway," he thought.

The men landed and slid to the side of the road. One man was killed instantly; the other man was severely injured and lay unconscious for several minutes. When he came to, he had no idea how long he had been there. However, he did know he would be dead soon without help. As he assessed the damage to determine if he could get up, he heard what sounded like a vehicle approaching. He knew it would be better if he didn't move, but if he didn't get to the side of the road, no one would be able to help him. The pain was almost overwhelming as he pulled himself up to the side of the road to see who was coming.

Steve Roy was moving more cautiously than his target. He

would not be surprised to find Thompson's truck wrapped around a tree. He hoped it would not end that quickly for the bastard. Then he saw the man by the road. He looked dead at first, and Roy was going to continue his pursuit when he saw the man raise a hand momentarily. He knew this was Thompson's man but figured he had been lied to like most of Thompson's men and was now finding out what kind of man he was working for. Roy couldn't drive past. In moments, he stopped, was out of his truck, and headed over to this man with a medic kit. The man couldn't talk at the moment, but he recognized Roy. The look in his eye said he expected to die now.

Instead, Roy leaned down and asked him, "Thompson do this?"

The man nodded slightly.

"Yeah, let me see if you're gonna live," said Roy, and he began checking the man's injuries. "What's your name?" he asked to keep the man talking.

The man struggled to speak and coughed slightly. "Ryan Williams, Sir."

"Well Ryan, you've got two broken legs. I will have to splint you in a bit, try not to move." Roy worked fast and continued talking to the man. "You also have two broken ribs, and it looks like you dislocated your shoulder. I will not be able to help with that until I am sure your ribs won't puncture your lungs. I am more worried about internal injuries. I will call in an extraction team for you. If you survive this, tell everyone how Thompson did this to you. I know he told that last crew he was working with me but just know that I would never send a man working for me into a mission like this without an exit plan."

Williams listened and nodded; he was amazed that Roy stopped to help him. He pointed to his companion. "What about Matthews?"

Roy looked where he pointed, looked back, and just shook his head. Williams nodded and closed his eyes. He wanted to pass out. Roy stayed by his side, talking to him to keep him alert, waiting till his extraction crew arrived.

44

Caleb and Frank

"Where is the Chief?" asked Frank.

"Not sure," Caleb was looking out at the woods. "I expected he would be back after those men left."

"Do you think they got him out there?" Frank was now looking out at the woods, not sure what he would see. He was worried about the Chief; there was a good number of bullets flying, and the Chief had been out in the midst of it.

Caleb was quiet for a few minutes. "No, I think I would know if he was gone. He may be checking to make sure all of them are gone."

"Do we wait?" Frank never took his eyes off the woods; he was still worried about the Chief.

"I will," Caleb said quietly, "I have the feeling that you will be needed up at the Chief's cabin soon. Something was going on there. Go make sure they got out." Caleb paused and looked over at Frank. "Be careful, I'm starting to like having you around."

Frank turned and looked at Caleb. Caleb's eyes showed trust and briefly glazed as if he was lost for a moment in a memory from long ago. The man's eyes then turned hard and cold again. "You better get going. I will wait for the Chief and meet you there."

Frank hesitated a moment but got up and walked through the passage. He would go back up the mountain to check on the kids.

45

The Chief Sees Roy

The Chief had been moving through the woods. Now that the assault was over, he didn't want to risk some innocent person being injured. So, as he moved, he released and disarmed all the traps Caleb had set.

He followed the path the last two men had taken in their flight. He came to the edge of the woods and saw Steve Roy tending to the injured man. He raised his weapon to prepare, but the wind spoke to him. He hesitated, then the birds flew down and circled around Steve Roy and the injured man. The Chief lowered his weapon, and the birds flew back into the trees. The Chief remained hidden and listened to what the man was saying; he observed the man tending to the wounds and calling a support team.

Roy stiffened; he had seen the birds and heard the change in the sounds of the trees. The wind through the trees was almost like voices.

He felt rather than heard the voices speaking to him:

Someone's watching.

He looked into the woods, knowing someone was there

though he could see none.

"Sit tight, Williams. My team will be here shortly. I need you alive," said Roy. "You are going to be my second corroboration that I am not on this job."

"What did Thompson tell you about these kids?" he asked.

Knowing he would survive, Williams had been able to relax and found he could speak with some difficulty. "We were told to kill them. Thompson said they were terrorists, and we had to take them all out. Now I don't believe him. I hope they are okay."

Don't worry," he said, "I got to the kids before Thompson could do anything. They are safe now—she is moving them." He said that last bit more to the woods than to the man on the ground.

The Chief heard this as he moved further back into the woods. He'd heard the other voices as well; this was something new. He would have to discuss this with Caleb and Sunshine. He turned and headed back to the cabin, no longer concerned that this man was at his back. They would need to follow Sunshine as soon as possible; he thought he knew where she would go.

46

The Wolf

Sunshine was riding through the woods, leading the way on a little-used trail. It was not as quick going as they had come from her cabin earlier, but they would not be seen on this trail. The girls were on one horse, Annie behind Sarah ducking under the overhanging branches. Tom was on the smaller horse Sunshine had brought—bringing up the rear. He had the shotgun at the ready and was holding the reigns with his other hand. He had learned how to ride quickly under Sarah's tutelage.

They had left Scott tied to the chair. Sunshine had made sure he understood that the woods would not let him go and that he was to remain where he was until the Chief returned.

When the woman led the kids away, Scott had briefly considered breaking free until he heard the sound of the wolf stepping in the back door. He could see it was staring at him. When he tried to move, it gave a low growl and stepped closer. When he stopped moving, the wolf stopped, but it kept staring at him. He decided to wait.

Frank observed the Chief's cabin. He wanted to be sure all was okay. He followed the path with his weapon at the ready position moving from cover to cover till he was confident the area was clear. He could see that two of the horses and the donkey were gone. Only the old man's and the Chief's horses remained in the corral. He followed the tree line around the clearing to the back. He stepped into the clearing at the corner of the cabin and quickly moved to the wall.

Inside the cabin, the wolf's ears perked up. It kept its eyes on Scott as it slowly backed out the door, then with a final growl, turned and looked at Frank as he came around the corner.

Frank froze, staring back at the wolf for a moment—shocked by the intelligence shining through the beast's eyes before it turned and ran into the woods. Frank moved forward and stepped through the door to find the man sitting still tied to the chair.

"Did you see it too? Is it gone?" the man asked.

Frank nodded, never moving his weapon from the man.

"I was told to wait here for the Chief. I tried to get up, and that wolf just walked in. Every time I tried to move, it got closer. Was it real?"

Frank nodded again. "Yeah, it was real; I saw it too. Who are you?"

"Call me Scott. You're sure it's gone?"

"Yeah, It's gone," said Frank. "You were supposed to wait for the Chief; you can sit right there till the Chief gets here."

"Fine by me. The last time I tried to move, she sent a wolf. I don't care to find out what she sends next," Scott replied. "Do

I have to stay tied up?"

"I think that's best for now," said Frank. "They will be along in a bit."

47

Caleb and the Chief

Caleb was cleaning and reloading his weapons when the Chief entered the cabin. Caleb looked up from his task, his hands never stopping as they followed the same motions they had performed many thousands of times before. He greeted the Chief and was about to return his attention to the weapons when he caught the look in the Chief's eyes. Only then did he pause in his task, turning his full attention to the Chief.

"What is it?"

"Chosen, there has been a strange occurrence by the road." The Chief stepped over and picked up a weapon from the table before continuing. He started disassembling and cleaning the Remington while Caleb remained silent, waiting for the Chief to continue.

"There has been a sign that we cannot ignore." The Chief continued cleaning the weapon as he gathered his thoughts before continuing. "The man that was our enemy..." he paused for another moment, "he appears to no longer be our enemy. I witnessed him by the road receiving directions from the spirits. He was speaking to one who we recently were fighting.

The man was not involved in this attack. He was trying to help this man but was speaking to the trees, birds, and animals... to me."

Caleb slowly resumed cleaning his weapon as he thought about this news. "Can we trust this? Should we trust this?"

"I believe he has chosen a new path. He is no longer hunting the children; rather I believe he is now hunting those who would harm them."

They fell silent as they completed cleaning the weapons.

"We need to speak to him; something is different now. I sense something I have never felt before. We should return to our family and make our plans," the Chief said as they finished.

Caleb nodded. "Let's pack it up then." He gathered his weapons and loaded his gun belts with the spare ammunition he made. They worked together to load up the horses, and they headed out. As they left Caleb had the thought that he might never be back to this cabin again. He looked back, expecting the forest to have begun growing in and reclaiming the clearing as happened when he left the cave.

Instead, his cabin was still there—no sign of trees, weeds, or animals reclaiming his old home. This calmed him some. Perhaps he would see this place again before he was done. Part of him rejoiced that his cabin was still there; yet another piece of him was saddened that he may not be granted his final rest. The Chief sensed more than saw what was going through Caleb's mind.

"Caleb, do not despair. Your time as Chosen will not be eternal. You have served faithfully and honorably, and when the time comes, you will receive your rest."

Caleb turned his eyes away from his cabin back to the Chief. The pain in his eyes cleared as they continued on their way.

"Thank ye, Chief," he said, then said no more as they rode back to the Chief's cabin.

48

Sunshine—Teaching and Learning

Sunshine led them up the mountain past her cabin and continued. Annie thought they were going to stay there but said nothing as they continued further. Sunshine would call a halt from time to time and go back several paces, chanting.

Then as Annie watched, the trail seemed to close behind them. She knew this was something she would learn. Sarah kept looking at Tom, occasionally giving him pointers and praising him for his riding abilities. They didn't seem to notice what Sunshine was doing.

Annie wondered how long it would take her to learn. As Sunshine passed, she smiled at Annie and winked. Annie felt rather than heard Sunshine speaking:

Not long, if you learn the names quickly.

They came to another turn on the trail. Sunshine's donkey stopped. He wouldn't proceed further. Sunshine looked up and saw what was bothering the donkey. A large hornet's nest was above the trail she wanted to take them down. They were active and agitated by an animal that had tried to break into their nest for the larva. Sarah saw them too. She jumped down, walked ahead of the donkey, and stood directly under the nest. The hornets flew around her for a minute or two then flew back up to the nest. They did not return to the ground.

Sarah motioned for the group to pass. First, Annie came on the horse, followed by Sunshine on her donkey. Tom was the last one, and as he passed, Sarah stood looking up at the hornets. Once all were through, she rejoined them and climbed back onto the horse.

Sunshine smiled at her, "I have seen very few who have the gift to calm an angry colony. If I am able, I would like to learn that from you."

Sarah frowned slightly. "If I knew how I would gladly show you, but I don't know why I can do that. Bees have never wanted to hurt me."

Sunshine smiled at her. "Nevertheless, I will learn from you."

Sunshine spoke more frequently as they moved further up the mountain. She was giving them names of animals and plants as they passed—not the names they had known from childhood but older names that seemed to hold power. Occasionally she would address Tom to show him something that she said would be important for him to know. After several hours they arrived at a small group of cabins. They looked like an abandoned campground, except the cabins were not in disrepair. Sunshine put Tom in the first cabin and had him tie his horse between his cabin and the next one. There she tied her donkey and had the girls pick if they wanted to stay in their own cabin or share one of the remaining.

Sarah and Annie decided to share the next cabin. They tied the horse they rode to the side of the cabin as Sunshine directed. They brushed the animals and fed them grain. They brought water from the pump and filled the trough by each cabin.

Sunshine turned to tom. "You go to the edge of the woods. Let me know if you can see anyone following. Stay quiet and listen. The animals will tell you if someone is there."

Tom quietly walked over to where they had emerged. He was surprised by how far down the mountain he could see. There was no one following that he could see. He listened. The animal noises were steady and calm. Nothing seemed to be bothering them. He waited there at the wood line, looking down through the trees and listening. He remained long after he would have if he were by himself. He wanted to be doubly sure now. The girls depended on him.

Sunshine took the girls to the other side of the cabins. There she showed them the full circle of the clearing. "They keep these cabins ready for people in need," she said. "They will know someone is here. We may have a visitor or two in the morning. Let me speak with them first. Right now, they are watching us and Tom in particular." The girls looked over at Tom. He was keeping his vigil still, turning his head side to side, listening carefully. Sunshine smiled.

"He is doing well; they will accept him."

Tom turned back to them and slowly walked back to Sunshine. "I didn't hear anyone back there. The woods sounded calm."

"Good," she said, "go to your cabin now. Open the windows and listen to the sounds. Learn the way the woods sound now. If it changes, pay attention, the woods will give warning before your eyes."

Tom nodded and thanked her. He then hugged Annie and Sarah and went back to his cabin. There he opened the windows and sat on the bed and listened. He listened till he could almost understand the language of the woods, then was asleep before he knew.

Sunshine had taken the girls to their cabin and settled them in. "Do not leave your windows open. That is the lesson for Tom. It would be best if you girls rested up. We will be starting early tomorrow." She then turned and walked out the cabin door, leaving them to get ready for bed.

Sarah turned to Annie after they were alone and said. "How can I teach anyone how the bees don't sting me? I don't even know why."

Annie smiled at her.

"I think with Sunshine and the Chief helping us, we may learn together. Let's do what she said and get some sleep."

49

Scott

Back at the Chief's cabin, Scott remained tied and did not struggle in his bonds. Johnston had said he would remain bound till the others arrived. But, after his experience with the wolf, he was okay with staying put.

He was not sitting idly waiting, though. His mind was going over what Roy had said and on Thompson bugging out and leaving him behind. He was considering ways he could make Thompson pay. Most of his ideas involved working with Roy against Thompson or even working with Johnston, if they would accept him. He was considering ways to convince them but knew there was a much lower chance of them taking him since he came after the girls armed. Johnston was not talking to him, so he remained silent and waited.

They maintained their silent companionship till Caleb and the Chief arrived. Caleb entered first from the front door, and the Chief went to care for the horses.

As he entered, Caleb noted the man tied to the chair. He looked to Frank and asked, "Will you be introducing me to our guest?"

"This is Scott; he was here when I got here. Sunshine had a wolf guarding him. So I figured we should leave him where he is till you and the Chief got here.

The Chief came in and looked at the man, then to Caleb, then turned to Frank and asked, "What do we have here?"

"Sunshine left him for us. The kids are away safely; we will need to catch up on our own. But, before we go, we need to discuss what to do about our new friend," Caleb said.

Frank said, "Scott, are you loyal to the man who abandoned you here?

"Not really," he replied, "but if I turn on him, it is unlikely I will ever get another job."

"I understand that. What if I had a way for you to be anonymous?" Frank looked into Scott's eyes, trying to read him. There was no change, no indication that he was even considering an offer. "You know you are not getting out of this one," he said.

"I know, but I can't be the one to break that trust first."

Frank smiled. "What if it is made known that your boss abandoned you because he was a coward."

Scott looked back at all three of them. "Can you do that?"

Frank nodded, saying, "I know someone who can get the word out quietly but in a way that everyone will know your boss is implicated, not you."

Scott then nodded. "If you can confirm that, I will speak."

"Are you working for Roy?" Frank asked.

"No, Roy would've had an exit plan for us and wouldn't have run out on me. He was here. He brought the boy back and helped that woman get the kids out of here. He chased off Thompson."

Frank watched him as he spoke. There was no hesitation,

no deceit. He was sure this man was truthful. "So everyone we have in custody has told us they have been working for Roy." He leaned forward. "Are you telling me Roy is not involved?"

"I know he was involved initially, but now they are trying to set him up to take the fall. My orders were that we were supposed to kill them all. Then at the first sign of trouble, he bugged out on me." Scott then leaned forward as well. "No more till you have my protection."

"I will arrange it," said Frank. He then turned to Caleb and the Chief. I will have to bring him down off the mountain to bring him in. Your cabin location will be public knowledge after that."

The Chief nodded. "I will not need it any longer. Let them come, and they will find an empty shell." He then turned and walked outside.

Caleb said, "Will you be able to get him there yourself?"

Frank looked at the man. "Sunshine sent a wolf to keep him in line; I am sure it is still there. I will be able to get him taken in. You go after the kids. I will call it in once you are gone."

Caleb nodded and went out after the Chief. The Chief had saddled the horses and had their roll packs tied to the saddles. Caleb and the Chief mounted and rode to the main path down the lane. They were out of sight of the cabin before they changed direction and the Chief took the lead. He suspected where Sunshine went and would lead Caleb to them. As they rode away, he turned them off the path. They faded away into the trees.

50

The Elders

Tom's sleep was filled with dreams of animals watching in the woods. They were pacing like sentinels but making normal sounds of just living their lives. As they were watching, he heard a change in the distance. It was a very slight change, almost unnoticeable at first, but he somehow sensed it.

The change was moving towards them; the animals in that area went silent as if letting something pass, then they resumed vocalizations, although slightly more urgent as if giving a warning. Tom struggled to get up. He looked out the window to see a light coming through the woods like a flashlight shining down. As he watched, the light drew closer. He tried to make out who it was. He couldn't speak. He tried to move to the door but tangled his feet in the blankets and fell to the floor. As he lay there, he thought he heard a voice saying to go for the girls first.

Suddenly he woke from his nightmare and sat bolt up in bed. He was confused for a moment before realizing he had been dreaming. He calmed himself down and looked out the window. There was no light, no men, and no voices. He was about to lay back down when he heard the sounds of the woods change. Just like in his dream, he heard the slight change as the animals and insects of the woods indicated where the intruder was coming from.

He slipped his feet over the edge of the bed and put on his shoes. He had left his clothes on so didn't have to waste any time with that. He stepped over to the door and listened before cracking it open. There was no one there, so he slipped out and went over to Sunshine's door using the shadows as cover. He scratched at her door quietly. He was surprised at how quickly she answered.

"Someone is coming through the woods. I heard the change in sounds."

Sunshine looked over his shoulder and listened as well. "You have done well Tom, go over to the girl's cabin and wait in the shadows by the horses."

She stepped out and headed towards the woods. Tom slipped through the shadows to the girl's cabin. He waited by the horses where the building blocked the moonlight as Sunshine had instructed. He listened. The approaching change of sound was unnerving him as he wished he knew what was causing it. Suddenly he felt the change in the air as the noise of the woods suddenly went silent in the area near the cabins. He then heard voices speaking. He heard Sunshine answer.

Though he could not understand what they were saying, he felt the woods come back to life and peace returned. The voices sounded happy. Then Sunshine came back with two elders from her tribe. She introduced Tom to them in their language but did not give Tom their names. The man was very old but looked strong. The woman looked to be a little older than Sunshine, and she smiled at Tom as she spoke. Sunshine answered her in English: "Yes, he heard you coming before I did, but to be fair, I told him to listen, and he had his windows open."

The old man smiled then. "You did well bringing them along. We did not even see your trail. We only knew that the woods were guarding the camp, so we came to see. We will be staying tonight and will be happy to meet your charges more formally in the morning." He then turned to Tom and held out his hand. "Pleased to meet you, Tom. You can call me Shashtsoh, and this is Awinita." Tom shook his hand and then nodded back at Awinita as she had to him when introduced. The old man smiled and turned back to Sunshine. "Set him to guard us again tonight. I will trust him." They took up residence in the cabin across from Sunshine.

Sunshine walked with Tom back to his cabin. "You did very well. He pays you great honor. Go back to your vigil and listen carefully." She turned and went back to her cabin. Tom waited till her door closed, then quietly stood listening. The woods were speaking calmly to him. He relaxed and returned to his bed. He lay there listening to the woods, trying to recognize the animals he was hearing.

Again, he was almost sure he could hear what the animals and insects were saying as he fell asleep.

51

Thompson

Thompson was in his headquarters, his hand stitched up and bandaged. He would have to shoot left-handed now till this healed. He could do it—he prided himself on being able to shoot nearly as well left-handed as right but wasn't about to take on Roy by himself with only one good hand.

He had been making calls on the encrypted satellite phone, trying to hire more men most of the day. He needed to rebuild his team quickly. He was not getting the responses he was hoping for. Several had not even answered. The few who did answer said they were otherwise engaged and hung up on him. The men he was able to hire were good but certainly not in the top tier. He was disappointed but would have to make do with only the seven men who had agreed to join him.

He chose Carter to be his second. He was the best of this bunch and would use his talents.

Thompson was deep into planning his next steps, sure Scott was dead by now. Roy would have had him trapped in that cabin, and Thompson would have killed Scott if he were Roy. He used that in his recruiting calls, telling those who knew

Scott that Roy had killed him. This brought some of them on board with the attitude that Thompson wanted; they would go hunt for Roy and those traitors he was protecting. Thompson would take the men and go back to that damn cabin. He knew they would find the remains of his last team, but he would use them as proof of Roy's guilt—motivating them to go after Roy, Johnston, and those damn kids. Anyone protecting them would be dealt with at the same time. He never gave a second thought to the older men or that woman with the children. His thoughts were that Roy was slipping if an old man could get the better of him. Thompson knew he wouldn't fail where Roy did.

Some of the men he had hired that day were beginning to arrive. He had them stock up and pack their kits. He was building himself up in his head, repeating his story to himself to the point he believed it himself. He would lead these men into battle against those old men and take Roy out himself when he found him. He forced himself to believe he was better than Roy and that he would succeed. He wanted to stand in front of these men like George C. Scott did in *Patton*. That desire was strong, but he had to hold himself back; he knew the men would see it as a stunt. So he played it through in his mind as he wanted it to be and smiled to himself. His daydream would have to suffice for now. After he won, he could make his speech, and they would have to listen to him.

52

Jamison

Caleb and the Chief were gone. Frank and Scott waited for a good hour before Frank made the initial call from his Satphone. His preliminary report was enough to set up the meeting with Jamison. Then they headed out. Frank took them back down the mountain to the same safe house near the park. He guessed no one would suspect he would use the same place after it had been compromised and his gamble paid off.

The house was open, and the surveillance equipment had been removed. It was no longer in use as a safe house. He and Scott entered and searched the interior to make sure. Once they were certain, Frank took out his phone and waited for the secure signal to sync up. He dialed the number and hid the encryption code. The conversation was quick and gave only the minimum details, just enough to ensure that Jamison could meet with them. Frank and Scott then changed clothes and disguised themselves before leaving to meet with Jamison. They caught the bus to town, not sitting next to each other, but they both changed busses at the same stops.

After the third stop, Frank went into a parking garage and

walked up the steps to the 4th floor. He climbed into a small car and drove it around to the opposite side of the building to exit. There when he stopped for traffic, Scott climbed in. They proceeded through the streets, and after about an hour, they arrived at the site. They parked the car on the road.

Frank dropped a special disk into the coin slot for the meter and turned the knob. The timer went one notch past the full-time mark and locked in place. Every parking enforcement officer would see the parking paid in full and bypass this car. It would remain until the next agent needed it. When the car moved away, the radio signal that kept the meter full would go out of range, and the disc would drop through and disappear into the quarters collected. The material would crumble to dust as the quarters were collected and dumped into different bags.

Frank led Scott into a nondescript building and entered the third elevator. Frank pressed the third-floor button five times then rapidly pressed a sequence of numbers. The elevator dropped down past the basement and opened into a sub-basement office. Jamison was there with a team to receive Scott.

He told them everything he knew, easily clearing Roy of all but the initial assault on the family that took out the parents. He implicated Thompson as the one who was directly responsible for most of the events after. He told of conversations he overheard that implicated someone inside was directing Thompson. Scott's description backed up Jamison's suspicion of Wells. It wasn't enough to go forward yet, but it was sufficient for Jamison to put a team on Wells to monitor his activities. Jamison's team would dig deeper now, and something would have to stick.

Jamison knew he should keep Frank and Scott in seclusion, but he couldn't do that now. Frank and Scott stated they were going back to ensure Thompson failed. If Wells was directing Thompson, he couldn't risk the internal teams. There was enough obvious evidence already showing that there were compromised agents on the inside. He still wanted Scott to remain and send Frank out, but they both argued against Scott staying. Finally, Jamison backed down and dispatched them with new satellite phones to keep in contact with him. He waited a good two hours before making his report. He followed protocol when suspecting someone; he reported to Forester requesting he send the information around the channels to bypass Wells. Forester agreed and sent the report two levels above Wells back to the office in Renton, Washington. From there, the report would be forwarded up to D.C.

53

Caleb and the Chief

Caleb and the Chief had continued up the trail, the Chief spotting signs that even Caleb could not follow—signs indicating that Sunshine had directed them this way. He was proud of his Granddaughter. She had covered their trail well. As he and Caleb followed, they had to go off the path around the tree that held the hornet's nest and pick it up past that point. They were careful not to disturb the insects.

It took all their skills on horses to go around the path; the terrain was rugged enough that the Chief wondered how Sunshine would have been able to get through. The kids would not have been able to ride around the same way as Caleb and he had done. But he saw no sign that anyone had come this way. It appeared as though Sunshine and the kids had just walked through the hornets' territory. They continued on until they reached the crest of the path. As the camp came into view below them, they paused. There were several people from the Chief's nation there. Usually, they only came to this place when a charity group came to provide aid to the tribes. The Chief knew that nothing of the sort was scheduled just then. He scanned the people and finally picked Sunshine out of the group. She saw him simultaneously and nodded to him, then tilted her head towards the cabins on the west side of the clearing. He led Caleb then around the perimeter. They stopped at the first cabin, where Tom greeted them.

"It's about time you guys got here. I have been 'watching' your approach for a while," he said. "I wasn't sure it was you at first, but Shashtsoh said it was you. He has been teaching me."

The Chief nodded and smiled. "Shashtsoh is here? That is good. He has always wanted to meet you, Caleb. He has been a great help to me with my family. His family has never shunned mine for our Shaman mixed blood."

Caleb looked at the Chief. He had never known about this part of the Chief's life. He was saddened that his friend had experienced this and disappointed with himself for never knowing in all these lifetimes. He again felt so different this time. He felt older but more part of the living world this time. As he thought of it, he found that he had become more a part of a family than he ever had before. He feared the inevitable pain of leaving them this time, as he always had to do when his task was done.

54

Quinn

After the attack at the cabin, Steve Roy had his men take the injured man to his medical team. They had taken care of him and then contacted Ward Jamison to tell him that they would turn him over when he was recovered. They would keep him safe until then and pass any information along as the man revealed it to them. Next, Roy had his men take the bodies of the other mercenaries out of the area and turn them over to Jamison. He trusted them to take care of it all; he told them to deal only with Jamison then to stand down. They were free and clear and would remain so. He was going to take full responsibility for this last mission.

If he was going to be taken down for this, he wanted his men to be out. Thompson and Wells would go down with him. His men had reluctantly agreed, and Roy had reloaded his weapons and ammo packs; almost as an afterthought, he grabbed his 50 caliber sniper rifle and a box of ammo for it. Roy then left them to return to the mountain. He drove to the Chief's cabin and hid his truck in the corral. He loaded up his pack and started up the slope. When he got to the end of the road, he paused. This was going to take too long. He found the going slow as he was weighed down with the full pack with multiple small arms weapons. The most difficult was the 50 caliber rifle, which weighed several pounds on its own. He went back up to the cabin, not wanting to take his truck—it would be too visible.

Roy walked around the cabin. There he found an electric ATV. Frank had left it there plugged into the solar charging box. He checked the charge and found the primary batteries fully charged. He was even happier when he noticed that it had dual sets of batteries. He would be able to ride nearly four hours before they ran out. He loaded his equipment on the back, climbed on, and headed out again. He found the trail the horses had taken. He followed the path, noting the passage of the Chief and the old man. The trail was challenging to follow from the seat of the ATV, but the voices in his head were beginning to help him find the signs of passage. He was getting too used to the voices, especially the one always calling him Buachaill. He was starting to rely on them; he had to force himself to keep his self-dialogue going as well.

As he moved along, he heard the old Irish voice again, "Well Buachaill, you better look ahead a bit. You're heading into a nest of trouble."

Roy looked up and saw the two large hornets' nests hanging just above head high just a few feet in front of him. He slowed and moved carefully around them keeping himself as silent as he could. After he passed them, he said quietly, "Thanks." He paused, realizing that he was now talking back to the voice. He shrugged, continued moving, and asked out loud, "Can I at least have your name? I like to know who I am talking to."

There was a long silence, and Roy thought perhaps he had

imagined it all—that he had begun to lose his mind. But then the voice responded:

"Call me Quinn."

Roy saw he was coming closer to a group of cabins. He pulled off the path, unloaded everything from the ATV, and lined it up on the ground. He pushed the vehicle under the cover of some brush, then set up the charger and ran the cables. The next morning the sun would start charging both sets of batteries. It would be slow charging in the middle of the woods, but enough light would be there to make this a viable escape vehicle for him. He stepped back and checked his work.

"Exit strategies, Quinn," he said quietly as he added more coverage to the ATV in the form of leafy sticks and branches.

"Always a good idea," came the reply.

Roy adjusted the cover for the ATV till he was sure no one would see it then picked up his packs and strapped them on his back. Lastly, he lifted the heavy 50 cal rifle and held it over his shoulder. He continued on foot sensing that he was close enough now. He moved around the woods about 75 yards away from the clearing around the cabins seeking an ideal position to set up.

55

Thompson

Thompson led his new team back to the old man's cabin. He kept Carter close to himself to ensure he had his back covered by someone with some skills. Thompson had been monitoring the news cycles and had seen no reports of bodies being found, and he expected them to be there still. He wanted to use them to motivate these men further. While moving through the woods, he kept his surprise in check as they approached and found no dead men to show. The two he ran down should have been at the side of the path. He checked the area near the trail, and it appeared that the ground had been swept. He took his men into the woods, directing the men on point to keep their eyes open. He held himself back just far enough that he felt he could retreat but close enough to the front that the men with him would not notice his reluctance. As they passed through the woods, they found evidence of a firefight. There were shell casings and blood. They found the traps sprung, some with blood still on them but disabled so they would not be able to spring again.

Thompson turned to the team. "You see? This is where your

friends died. Our targets hid the bodies but didn't have time to clear all the evidence. Stay cautious and hidden now; we need to take them."

He hoped he could still use this as motivation. He was careful to say 'take them' only and not 'take them out' so afterward he could say that he didn't order the kids to be killed. He never forgot to cover his ass.

Thompson and his men continued to move slowly forward till they reached the clearing. The cabin showed several bullet marks. Some of the windows were gone entirely, while others were broken with small pieces of jagged glass still hanging in the frames. They found more signs of men dying near the cabin. Still, no bodies. They searched the perimeter of the clearing and saw no sign of life. Thompson sent his point man to check the cabin. He came back, reporting it was empty. The place was cleaned and, except for the broken windows, looked as if nothing had happened inside. Thompson hid his confusion as he ordered his men to search the woods for signs of what direction their target had fled. It did not take long for them to find the path.

Thompson knew where this path led but let his point men follow as he struggled to figure out where the bodies had gone. He would have left them there or buried them. There were no bodies and no fresh graves.

Where are they?

He reasoned that if they took the time to take care of the bodies, that was time he had gained in the pursuit. He figured they were closer now than they might have been. They might even catch them at the next cabin.

56

Jamison

The bodies were being examined in the agency morgue, and Ryan Williams was now secured in the agency hospital. He had been interviewed by Roy's men and now had been speaking directly with Ward Jamison over the phone, and his statements combined with those of Scott would fully clear Francis Johnston and cemented in his mind that Wells was involved. He would bypass Wells with this report and keep him in the dark. Jamison wanted to string him along till he was so exposed that he wouldn't be able to weasel his way out of it. He suspected Wells would turn evidence as even in meetings; he was always covering his ass. He wasn't the type that would go down by himself. Jamison wished that Frank had brought Roy in and Scott had stayed, but they had told him the situation prevented this. They were still out there, and he knew they would find where the kids were. They had to protect these kids. Jamison wanted to go out in the field with Johnston and bring these asshats hunting the kids down, but he knew if he did, then whoever was pulling the strings in this menagerie would be tipped off. They would distance themselves from it or start taking out subordinates before they could talk. So he had to proceed with caution.

Jamison reread his report. He wanted to be sure it was airtight before he sent it along. He also wanted to ensure it did not indicate anyone above Wells. He wanted to keep from documenting that he suspected anyone of a higher rank. So he left it open for them to suggest it, but it did not contain any evidence of anyone other than Wells running the show. This he hoped, would cause them to let their guard down a little and maybe make a mistake and expose themselves.

Satisfied, he put everything in the box, sealed it, and handed it to his assistant with strict instructions for her to take it directly to Jim Forrester. Forrester had backed him on this investigation and had kept everything secret. He could trust Forrester to read between the lines and understand what Jamison was not saying.

57

New Family

The feast with the Chief's tribe was terrific. They had spent much of the time sampling foods and listening to stories told by the Elders. They had brought supplies and provisions. They danced late, and Tom and Sarah had even sneaked off to her cabin for a time. Tom had told her how he felt. She had been delighted and had told him she loved him. That night had been the best he ever had. He knew he wanted to marry her and would find a way. They had a dance that welcomed Sarah, Annie, and Tom into the tribe as new family members. Shashtsoh taught Tom the steps, and Awinita taught the girls. The gathering had broken up near midnight, and the Chief's people returned to their village, promising to accept them all into their community whenever they wished. It had been a great night, and Tom had walked the girls back to the cabin. Annie looked at them as they walked. She knew what was going on, and she smiled. She felt she had a new sister now, and she was content. After settling the girls into their cabin, Tom returned to his own. He prepared for bed and made sure his windows were open, as Shashtsoh had taught him. He lay there listening to the woods settling in for the night. As he was lying there, his thoughts kept going to Sarah. It was a struggle to get his mind clear and settled for a time. Finally, he was able to focus and synchronize his mind with the sounds of the woods. As he listened, at the moment he almost believed he could understand the words on the wind, he fell asleep. Yet even in this sleep, he was alert to the sounds of the woods.

Tom woke with a start. The sounds had changed momentarily and were now settling back down. 'Someone's out there,' he thought. He climbed from his bed to the floor and crawled to the corner of the room before standing as Shashtsoh had instructed. Here he was in the darkest corner of the cabin and could see out the windows to the woods. He could also hear the sounds of the woods better as the acoustics of the room focused sound to this corner. The sounds of the woods were close to normal, but he felt something was off. Someone was out there. He knew it, but he could not tell where they were. He had to get to Caleb and the Chief in the next cabin. He slid back to the floor, slipped into his jeans, and pulled his shoes back on. He stayed crouched down as he went to the door and cautiously stepped out. It was darker here on this side of the cabin, and he waited for his eyes to adjust before moving. He kept listening carefully for any sound. Then, hearing nothing, he ventured through the shadows of the night over to the cabin that the Chief and Caleb were using. He scratched on the door as the Chief taught him. The door opened a crack a moment later, and the Chief pulled him in.

"You heard it too?" the Chief asked.

"Yes," Tom said, "Someone is out there watching. They are not approaching, but they are not leaving either."

"Good job," said the Chief. "You are learning quickly. Could you tell from what direction?"

Tom hesitated, he had just been taught how to judge the direction of sounds in the woods, but he had not remembered to do so. "Sorry, no. I didn't remember."

"Don't worry about it. You will remember next time," the Chief smiled, then stood and listened through the open windows. "I think I know who it is. I will make sure and report back. You stay with Caleb and keep the girls safe." The Chief slipped out into the darkness and disappeared into the shadows. Tom noticed that no sounds changed when the Chief passed.

"Relax, son," said Caleb. "The Chief is proud of you. He won't say it yet, but I been around him and his people for a long time. He considers you to be kin to him now. You, Sarah, and Annie are his grandchildren now. You will be safe with him when I am gone from this time and place."

Tom looked at him, wondering again at the life of this man. He hadn't thought about Celeb going away. It had never occurred to him that would happen; now, he felt the coming loss deeply. He was about to ask Caleb to stay when he felt, then heard, the change in the forest; something was coming. He listened to the birds and the insects. The nighttime conversations between the animals even stopped as whatever was coming passed. He could tell whoever was coming was approaching on the path that came in from the opposite end of the clearing near the roadway where cars and trucks would come up to the settlement. "Someone's coming up the roadway," he said as the Chief slipped back into the door.

"We have our shadow back," the Chief said.

Caleb nodded, turned to Tom, and smiled. "You head over and knock on Sunshine's door. Let her know we will have new arrivals and let her know about our shadow in the woods." Caleb looked back down the path at the car approaching with the two men in the front seat. "If she hasn't already, have her wake the girls. Our day is starting early; the sun is almost up, so the sleep they have had will have to be enough."

Frank was driving, and the other man, Scott, was sitting in the passenger seat. Scott kept his hands on the dash in Frank's line of sight. He knew that they had no reason to trust him. After giving his statements to Johnston and Jamison, he heard what that kid Ryan Williams had said. When he heard that Thompson ran him down, he was shocked, then quickly moved to rage. He begged Johnston to let him come with him. He would not let this pass. Killing your own men like that just to cover your own escape? Thompson was an ass, but Scott never expected that. Now he wanted to make sure he paid for that. He had brought the radios and decrypt attachment to allow him to hear what Thompson's team was saying. He would be on the hunt now. The Chief stepped out and greeted them. Caleb stayed back in the cabin out of sight but kept watch through the window. He was acutely aware that their shadow was watching. The Chief had said it was Steve Roy and they might be able to trust him. Caleb had not decided yet. Roy was a dangerous man. He would approach that relationship with caution. The Chief then said, "There are others out there now, and Roy does not appear to be with them.

When Tom arrived at the cabin door, he knocked quietly. He had kept to the shadows and was almost convinced he had made it without being seen. He was surprised when Awinita answered. "The girls are ready; go get Shashtsoh from the water tower. Let him know we need him now. Sunshine and I will keep Sarah and Annie safe until you return."

Tom turned and again moved in the shadows past the cabins on the west side of the clearing till he reached the old water tower. There he whistled a bird call he had learned and was surprised how quickly the old Cherokee could swing over the rail and to the ground.

"Let's go meet our visitors Tom. You did well this morning. I was up only a few seconds before you. You are learning quickly."

"No, Shashtsoh, Awinita said to bring you back to her. We need to move the girls."

Shashtsoh looked back down the path to the car as it was coming in, then turned with Tom towards the girl's cabin as the car stopped near the horse corral. He started chanting, his deep voice vibrating in Tom's ears. Tom could feel the power in the old Indian's voice. The shadows around them seemed to close in as they moved.

58

Wells

Wells broke the seal on the secure inner office memo; his mole had sent just a few notes to him from the report that Jamison sent to Forrester. This junior-level employee sent only the pieces that seemed relevant to Wells according to the task they were given. Wells read the memo.

'*What the fuck!*' he thought.

He reread it a second and third time. It reported that one of Thompson's men was rescued from a mission and was talking. The part that struck Wells was that this man was saying his orders were to kill all the targets; no one was to be captured.

"GET IN HERE NOW!" he barked at the door.

The lead of his security detail came in and stood at attention. "Sir."

Get a car ready; load it up for a possible fight. We will be leaving as soon as we can get going."

"You want the van? A car won't fit us all, sir."

"No Zeke, just me and you are going."

Wells then looked directly into the man's eyes. "Priority classified mission, go get the car. I will be down straight away."

Zeke saluted and marched out. Wells grabbed his satellite phone and turned on the GPS ping application. He entered Thompson's phone in the app and initiated the scan. Wells had to stop that asshole. If that Abraham girl was injured in any way, everyone was going to be toast. That dumb fuck was going to get them all hanged. Just before he walked out the door, the Sat phone rang. Wells hesitated a moment before answering.

"When are you going to return my girl to me?"

"Mr. Abraham, I have just learned the location and am heading out to take care of this mess personally, sir." Wells waited a few moments for the man to answer. Wells was becoming impatient waiting for Abraham to speak again. When he was unable to take the silence anymore and was about to speak Abraham spoke again.

"You will return my daughter to me directly. If you fail to return her you will have nowhere you can hide."

Wells responded automatically, "Understood, sir!" It bothered him to call anyone sir, but at this moment, his reply was given without hesitation.

Abraham hung up almost before the obligatory 'sir.' Wells rushed out the back hallways to the waiting car. He was on his way down to the car when he received the secure message on his phone from Thompson. The report showed him that there was still time to fix this royal fuckup. He engaged the tracking and handed the target info to his driver.

"Follow this GPS ping," he told Zeke. "We have to stop that son-of-bitch before he gets us all killed."

They took off just under the speed that would automatically get them pulled over. He tried calling Thompson. The second time his call did not go through, he started to panic.

He dialed the number a third time.
'That fucker better answer his goddamn phone.'

59

Thompson

Thompson felt the Sat phone vibrate twice more and was doing his best to ignore it. He and his men were moving through the woods following the trails. One of these new men was an exceptional tracker and had found the path where the horses and the ATV had passed. His scout had been able to confirm the direction. Not far down the track, the horse prints disappeared. Only the ATV had continued on this path from that point. Even that vanished after several hundred meters. They were continuing on old animal trails and hiking paths. On the map, his other man had found the temporary lodges used by the Reservation for important visitors. He suspected that was their destination and was now deploying men to surround the site. He would approach from the roadway that evening when he was sure everything was in place. He had sent the secure dispatch to Wells the day before to let him know he would have them tonight. He planned his approach carefully. He had fewer men than he wanted, but it was the team he could get. They would have to do their jobs well for this to work. He was talking to all of them on his encrypted radios, checking to ensure they would be in place by late afternoon. He had planned a coordinated effort so they would be approaching from every direction. He wanted no escapes this time. He was informed that Johnston and one other man had arrived in a car; the scout had not seen who was in the car with him. In Thompson's mind, he was sure it was Roy—he had them all now. He wanted to hurry in but knew he had to give them time to get in place. He kept running through his plan in his mind. He could not see it failing; all he could see was that Roy and Johnston would pay.

The men had to be close to being in position now. He felt the phone buzz again and ignored it again. He clicked his radio mike in the predetermined sequence. The clicks started coming back in. Some of them were in place. Others were reporting they were still moving into position.

"Carter," Thompson said, "I am going in here," he pointed on the map. "You go in from this path. This will bring us out right behind the cabin where the girls were spotted. We get in there and capture them while everyone is watching out front. Then, we will be able to use them to flush the others out."

Carter wanted to use more men and suggested a few names. Thompson thought about it and reluctantly agreed. He sent the signals for the men to check in on the secure channel again. He informed them of the change and ordered them to sit tight. Carter stepped out and headed down the path to get the needed men. Thompson smiled; Roy was there, Johnston was there, that old man and the Indian were there. He could take them all out at once. These men believed him and were ready to kill them all. He was enjoying the feeling of pending victory when his thoughts were interrupted by the fourth time the satellite phone vibrated. Thompson finally looked at it. "Wells?" he whispered to himself, thinking, *'what the hell does he want now?'* He was so close. He ignored the call again and suited up in his Kevlar, holsters, and ammo belts. He was decked out and ready; it was only a matter of time.

60

Roy's Choice

Roy had been in place for a long time. He had watched the gathering from his hide. He watched the dance and watched the villagers leave. He had carefully staked out his position. He had a clear view down the mountain the length of the clearing through the middle of the cabins. He had his weapons clean and ready. He had checked the loads multiple times. He had been speaking with Quinn for the last several hours. Quinn had told him the story of the Chosen; Roy now understood why the old man was so good. He admired him and had a strong desire to meet him again as a companion rather than an adversary. Quinn had asked him about himself, and he had spoken freely. It was therapeutic to say it out loud. As he went through it all in this conversation, he recognized when he had lost his way. He knew he deserved to go down for all he had done; he knew he probably would, but not tonight, not this time.

He remained and watched the remaining people go to their cabins. He kept talking to Quinn to stay alert. He was the first to see Thompson's new team moving into position. He adjusted his radio to find the frequency till the radio in his ear crackled. He had them now. He tuned in the encryption and chuckled to himself, realizing that Thompson was using an old encryption that he used with Roy on past missions. Details that Roy wouldn't have missed if he had planned this raid. Now Roy was listening in and could co-ordinate his position to help as much as he could to protect the people in the cabins. He had seen when Tom left his cabin and moved stealthily over to one of the others. He was impressed at the skill the boy displayed. After he entered the other cabin, Roy looked around. He heard one voice on the radio confirming the position, and Thompson himself acknowledged it. Roy smiled; he hoped he would get the chance to take that ass out. The next report over the radio was when Frank Johnston was driving up the road with someone else they could not identify. He smiled when he heard Thompson reply stating that the second one in the car must be Roy.

He was surprised when he saw the Chief appear at the edge of the clearing, looking up at his location. Roy at first thought he was exposed, but then he saw the Chief turn his head slightly to his left. Then the Chief gave his left hand two taps before he turned and dissipated back into the shadows. Roy looked to his left and saw Thompson's man settling in. He heard that man check in and reply to sit tight and wait for the signal. He moved his scope left and right along the perimeter. He found almost all of Thompson's men. He knew he would have seen them soon enough, but that old chief had shown himself to Roy to point out the location of the closest one without revealing himself to them.

"Quinn, I have to meet that Chief. He is the best I have ever known at hiding himself."

"You will, Buachaill," came the answer as the car approached.

Roy watched Johnston pull up and get out. He waited and finally, the other man in the car got out. Roy saw it was Scott. He glanced back at Thompson's man to his left. That man recognized Scott and appeared to be surprised that Scott was there. Roy checked the other men he could see. Only this one had seen Scott from this end of the clearing. That man did not appear to be reaching for his radio yet. Roy hoped he wouldn't. He watched as one of Thompson's men came through the trees and took a man back with him. Roy rechecked the locations he had noted in his head. Three of Thompson's men were moving out back. He had almost missed it. They were heading back into the trees towards where Roy suspected Thompson had his camp setup. He would have to keep his eyes open now.

He whispered, "Quinn, I have been out here too long without sleep. I can't miss anything; keep talking to me; keep me alert."

The voice continued telling him of the Chosen, of the many different lives that had become one with the Chosen. As the voice spoke, Roy thought, '*I would choose this if it came down to it.*' At that moment, he felt a little more alert, and the fatigue began to recede.

Quinn spoke directly to him, "Buachaill, do you understand what would be required of you?"

Roy thought a moment, "Yeah, I would be trapped in the life as Chosen for as long as it takes to pay for this life I chose to live. First, I would have to answer the call without hesitation and do what is needed; then I would have to wait for the next call."

"And you would choose that freely?" the voice of Quinn asked, but there was a slight change in the voice as if it was more than just Quinn who asked.

Roy nodded, "Yeah, hell, I choose it now. I don't deserve any mercy for this life, but maybe I can atone for it."

At that moment, there was a gust of wind filled with many voices. Voices that sounded like prayers in multiple different languages. Roy was filled with the voices; he was filled with memories that were not his own. It was nearly overwhelming, and it felt like it lasted for hours. In reality, it was between one moment and the next. When Roy looked down from his perch, he could see the men pulling back through the woods. He felt a strange sense of wonder, excitement, and resolve. Thompson would not succeed.

In the cabin, Caleb suddenly stood; he turned and looked towards the mountain as if he could see through the walls. At that moment, he felt the voices; he had a sense of power being passed along, although he did not feel diminished, just shared. He turned back to the Chief. "Something has changed. He smiled, yet he didn't know why.

61

Wells

Martin Wells yelled at his phone as he again pounded Thompson's number. "That dumb fuck better answer me now."

He turned to look at Zeke, "We have to be nearly there by now! What's taking so fucking long?"

"Sorry, Sir, I should have prepped a Jeep for us. But, unfortunately, this car can't take this road at this speed."

Suddenly a wolf darted across the road in front of them. Zeke swerved and barely missed the animal, but the car's front wheel caught a rut, and the car was pulled off the road. Zeke regained control with a mighty effort and a string of curses before the next corner.

Wells stopped complaining about not going fast enough.

A large branch dropped on the road as they came out of the curve onto the next straightaway. Too close for Zeke to avoid, there was a loud crunch as they rammed the branch. A cloud of steam burst under the hood as Zeke barely stopped the car at the edge of the dirt road. The engine rattled to a halt, and they heard the wolf's howl behind them. The men sat there a moment, breathing hard. Wells picked the Sat phone back up from the floor and put it to his ear. It was still ringing on the other end. That dumb fuck Thompson still wasn't picking up. Finally, they both pulled their guns out and climbed out of the car.

62

Thompson

Thompson sent out more clicks signaling his men. Roy smiled; he knew the code. He heard the other men clicking to check in. He figured he better see if Thompson was still an incompetent ass. So he added his own click to check in.

Thompson listened to the check-in clicks when the Sat phone vibrated again. He counted the clicks and had just verified that the last men were finally in place. He was about to move when he heard one more set of clicks. He paused for a second as he wondered about it, then he made up his mind that the Sat phone vibrating threw his count off. So he set out to meet up with Carter's little team. In his mind, he saw only his success. They would be in and take them all out. It would be easy to stage the scene with Roy to look like Roy was responsible. It would be glorious!

Thompson met up with Carter and the men chosen to join them.

"Timing is everything, men," he said. "Radio silence now, men. Carter, have your team switch off their radios. We can't have any radio sound giving us away when we are there.

Switch back on when you have them and on your way out. You'll need to direct the cover fire for our retreat."

They went down the chosen paths and arrived at the back sides of the cabins. It was clear; it would be easy now. Thompson saw Carter and his men and signaled them to proceed.

They executed a stealthy approach from shadow to shadow. They arrived at the back of the cabin unseen. They checked the door. There was no lock.

Carter slipped in, leaving one man to watch the door and others ready to provide cover from the trees. Thompson kept watch on the other cabins. He had them now; his men were at the girls' cabin. He rechecked the place and saw when Carter entered. They had the women now. His thoughts were only on how great it would feel to kill Roy and Johnston. The time was now. He stood behind the tree and checked his body armor; he was taking no chances with his own life. His body armor was on and fitted—no stray bullet would get him. He called out to the cabins, "Alright, everyone, just keep your heads and leave your weapons down. No one needs to be hurt." He waited a moment and called out again, "Roy, I know you're in there. I know you can see that I have everything covered, front and back doors. You have nowhere to go. Step on out here, and let us get these kids back to Wells and into witness protection."

He waited, looking for some movement, then saw a curtain move from an open window. He turned to look in.

"Thompson, you ass," Frank yelled, 'what the hell are you doing?"

Thompson smiled, "I am taking care of business. Now send Roy out. I want to see his face when all Scott's friends take revenge on him."

Scott almost laughed. Then his radio clicked, and he put it to his ear.

"Scott?" said Roy, "you still have your own code for your team?"

"Yep," he replied.

Roy said, "I think this asshat told all these men I killed you. Can you send that signal out to your men out here?"

"Yeah," said Scott.

"Good," said Roy. "Switch over to channel 15 encrypt code IIa7. Let them know what an ass it is they are working for. Tell them to hold back if you can."

"Sure thing," said Scott. He then changed the channels and started sending the click signals. Thompson didn't notice, as he was still out there taunting Roy or Johnston. Instead, he was reveling in his moment.

Scott then switched over to his own channel and waited. Several of the men switched.

"Hi guys, what kind of bullshit has Thompson got you all into now?" Scott asked.

After filling them in on the situation, they all switched back and passed the word that Thompson was lying to them. The only ones they couldn't reach were Carter and his small team.

Thompson missed it all with his radio off.

63

Negotiations

At the same time Thompson was challenging Roy and Johnston to give up and come out, Carter was moving through the girls' cabin. His radio was still off so he could move silently. He listened to Thompson and Johnston talking outside and timed his next move. He slipped through the cabin and appeared to have arrived without being seen. He slipped silently through the door and moved from the backroom to the front. The girls weren't there. He was suddenly unsure of himself as he moved into the room, checked each bed, and looked in each corner. He felt a fog in his mind as if he was getting a migraine.

Carter took a deep breath; he could almost feel a vibration in his head that was clouding his thoughts. He looked around again; no one was there. They had been watching the cabins, and no one had moved out. He slipped back out the way he came. He looked both ways, counting the cabins to confirm he was at the right one. Finally, he made his decision and moved with his men to the next cabin at the end of the row. He listened carefully at the back door.

Thompson was getting giddy with the rush. He saw his men

leaving but didn't notice that they had left the cabin without the girls. He switched his radio back on and said, "Carter get those girls to our camp. I will meet you there shortly." He then yelled out to Johnston, "Carter has the girls now. He is taking them back to our camp," he turned back to the cabin. "Johnston, you better send Roy out; we won't be keeping the girls alive for long!" He then clicked the button on his radio to signal his men to be ready.

Roy focused his scope and adjusted his aim to account for the wind but could not pull the trigger. There was no clear shot on the men stalking the women. His shot would go through them and the cabin behind them. He wouldn't risk it. He then moved his sights back to Thompson who was backing out of the site. He heard Thompson give the orders and clicked the mic on his radio.

"Thompson, you ass. You think I can let you waltz out of here after being so stupid?"

Thompson jumped around a tree to put it between him and the cabin for cover, then turned to look back past the trunk to the cabin where he thought Roy was hiding. "What you gonna do? You got nothing in there to get through this." He laughed as he patted his chest.

"What about my 50 cal?" Roy asked.

Thompson hesitated a moment looked down at his chest, and saw the red dot of the laser site; he looked up at the mountain and back at the dot on his chest, it was the last thing he saw before the tree behind him exploded from the 50 caliber round that ripped through his chest.

The echo of the shot arrived moments after Thompson fell. Carter saw Thompson go down as he and his men scattered back into the woods. Carter switched his radio on, yelling,

"Why is there no cover fire? Where the fuck did that shot come from?"

A man near Roy replied while looking up at the brush from where the shot came. "I have a feeling that was Roy. I gotta let you know, sir, Scott isn't dead. Thompson lied to us; I think he set us up."

Carter was not ready to believe them till he heard Scott come over the radio. "It's true, Carter; this is Scott,"

"Scott, I'm surprised to hear from you; I was told you were dead," Carter replied.

"Yeah, I heard something like that before. You know Thompson was going to use you guys and leave you to clean up his mess or take the fall. That's what he did to me. Are you going to try to finish his job?"

Carter stopped, he had been second in command, and Thompson was not going to be giving any more orders. He looked up at the mountain, then back at the cabins.

"Get back to camp, men. We are pulling out."

64

Roy

Roy packed his gear and hoisted his bag on his left shoulder with the big sniper rifle already loaded and strapped to his right shoulder. He strode down the mountain into the camp and walked right by the other mercenary.

Roy nodded to him as he passed, then continued on as if he didn't care if he was there or not. The man saluted Roy after he was gone. Roy saluted without turning back.

The man turned and ran back along the pathways to their camp. They were bugging out, and he wasn't going to risk being left behind.

Inside the girl's cabin, there was movement from one of the corners. Annie and Sunshine stepped forward out of the shadows, and both reached forward at the same time. They each took a hand of Shashtsoh as his chanting faded. His eyes were rolled back, and he was unsteady on his feet. As his voice faded, the shadows in the room diminished, and the others were no longer hidden. Awinita had been chanting with him, and when his chanting faded, she ended hers as well. She stepped forward and, in a weak voice said, "He held onto the song too long. Help me get him to the bed. Tom, go get the Chief. We need his help quickly."

Roy entered the camp casually, taking in the layout from the closer view. His mind automatically reassessed the weak spots in the defense and built a plan to shore them up—creating exit paths depending on where the next threat approached. He paused as he walked past what was left of Thompson. The shattered trunk of the tree was no longer strong enough, and it had toppled over next to Thompson's body, effectively hiding it from the cabins.

He turned as Tom burst from the cabin and ran across the commons, calling out, "Chief! We need your help!"

The Chief stepped forward and ran towards the girl's cabin before Tom finished calling for him. Scott and the old man came out the door of another cabin and started moving in the same direction when they saw Roy and stopped. The old man turned his body to present the smallest target and was poised and ready to draw and fire any of the four guns he had hanging at his sides. Roy held up his hand, showing he was not a threat. Scott stepped between them. "Take it easy," he said. "We are all on the same side."

Caleb nodded his head, "Hello."

Roy nodded back, then from the recesses of memories that he knew were not his own, he found the name and said, "Pleased to meet you, sir."

Caleb stared at him a few moments before he turned and ran after the Chief. Scott walked over to Roy.

"I need to stow my gear and take care of this mess," he said as he tilted his head back at Thompson."

"This cabin's empty," said Scott. "Stow it there, and I'll help you with Thompson."

65

Shashtsoh

The Chief was leaning over Shashtsoh singing an old and powerful song; Sunshine was singing with him while holding Shashtsoh's hands. Awinita was too weak to join the song; she had given as much of herself to Shashtsoh as she could while he hid them. There had been no time to move the girls, and he had chosen to protect them himself. It would be dangerous for a young man to hold the chant that long hiding just himself, but Shashtsoh had hidden them all. Awinita was very proud of his courage. She prepared a tea for him while the Chief and Sunshine worked the calling, directing him back to his corporeal shell. Awinita turned to Tom, Sarah, and Annie. She listed the ingredients she needed and asked them to go get them quickly. "Shashtsoh will need this when he returns to restore his strength." They set off out the back of the cabin and were in the woods to gather the needed herbs and plants in a blink.

Gray was dancing around in the corral. He had been trying to warn them that more danger was coming. He could not help them from the corral. Finally, he figured out the gate and had just released the latch when he saw the girls heading down the path with Tom. He knew he had to get between them and the danger. He took off down a different path heading straight towards the danger he felt. He had to get there before it was too late.

66

Wells

The car was trashed. Wells had climbed out as the steam rolled from the engine.

"What the hell else could go wrong?" he said out loud.

He and Zeke had stepped to the front of the car to find the branch that had fallen in the road in front of them had gone through the radiator and damaged the belts on the front of the engine forcing them to proceed on foot from there. He had called for the agency to send a truck to get them and the car. Before the vehicle arrived, he had to get up this mountain and get that girl. As they moved up the road, they heard the sound of the 50 caliber shot ringing through the trees. They were far enough away that the direction was difficult to trace through the trees. Wells was still following Thompson's Sat phone's GPS location tracking signal. The signal had stopped moving since the sound of that shot. Wells was getting desperate and hurrying along faster than he should be moving in the shoes he was wearing, but he had to get there. His life depended on getting that Abraham girl out of there.

"Sir, there is a path here," Zeke said. "Looks like it leads up to the cabins we saw on the map. It should be quicker than going around on the road."

"Let's go then," said Wells as he turned back to follow his man up the trail. They soon came to a place where the path split and went at 90 degrees left or right. One way led up closer to the cabins, the other looked to head back towards their damaged car.

"We can get back quicker that way when we come out," Zeke said.

"Good, now let's keep moving," Wells said.

They set off towards the cabins.

67

Annie and Sarah

The girls had gathered most of the ingredients needed for Awinita's tea. They handed the bags to Tom. "Take these back and tell them we will be right back, there is one more item we need, but she can get started with those. We will be right back."

Tom turned and ran back with the bags. He brought them into the clearing and was striding through the center of the clearing between the cabins where he met Caleb.

"Where are the girls?" Caleb asked.

Tom froze a moment. "Right down the path, they were coming right behind me."

Caleb looked down the path and back at Tom; they both turned to head down the trail. Caleb said, "No, You take those to Awinita now; they need it." He then turned and called out, "Roy!"

Steve Roy looked up and saw Tom running back to the cabin and Caleb heading down the path. "This doesn't look good," he said.

"I got this; you go," said Scott.

Roy took only his M-16 and the pistol strapped to his hip and met up with Tom as he returned from the cabin.

"The girls," said Tom.

Roy nodded and took off after Caleb. He was moving faster than he had ever been able to before. Finally, he came to the fork in the path. Caleb was on one knee, checking the signs. "Someone has the girls," he said. "They're taking them down this path."

Roy nodded and took the lead.

Wells couldn't believe his luck. The girls had stepped out of the woods onto the path behind them. They had a bag with herbs and stood there staring at the gun the younger man had pointed at them.

"Girls, I am so glad I found you," said the older man. "I am Martin Wells. You're Sarah Abraham, right? I was sent by your father to get you out of here."

He took hold of her arm. Zeke took Annie, and together they forced them down the path towards their coming ride. Wells thought he had finally caught a break. The girls were difficult and were not cooperating at first, but when Zeke threatened to leave Annie's body behind, they calmed down. They were moving along quickly now, and Wells felt they would be back just at the right time to meet the coming team.

Suddenly the shadows on the side of the path ahead of them erupted, and a large horse stepped out, barring their way. He had wild eyes that frightened Wells. He yelled at the horse to get it moving, but it would only step back and forth on the path blocking them every time they moved forward.

"Kill that beast," Wells told his man.

Roy caught up with them at that moment and called out,

"Hold it, Wells."

Wells and his man turned, keeping the girls between themselves and Roy.

"Roy, good to see you. I have the girls; we can proceed as planned," said Wells.

"Not gonna happen, Wells; you set me up." Roy's voice was steady and robust.

Zeke felt fear in his bowels. He brought his gun closer to Annie's head. There was a sudden movement to his left. As the man turned, his cheek tore open and exploded in pain as Gray's hoof came down on his face. He fell to the ground unconscious. Annie ducked forward as the man fell then turned back to help Sarah. Gray again placed himself between the bad man and the escape down the path. Gray was angry and kept moving, keeping him from being able to leave.

Wells kept Sarah in front of him as he backed up to a tree so the horse couldn't get to him. Roy was only 35 feet from them now. He took aim at Wells but couldn't shoot with Sarah in the way. Wells had his gun to her back and was ducking behind her as he backed around the tree further. Annie followed calling out to Sarah.

Roy followed as well and kept Wells in sight.

"You can't Roy; I'll kill her before you can get to me," Wells threatened.

Roy looked at him. Caleb came around the corner with his bow drawn and the arrow notched.

Tom followed. "Sarah!" he called.

Sarah had tears in her eyes, but she tried to remain calm. Tom and Annie were here, and they had Caleb with them. Somehow she had to get away from this man.

She heard the sound of her rescuers, just above the level of the men's voices as they talked. They were close; she caught Annie's gaze, then looked up with her eyes. Annie looked up and saw them too; she touched Roy's arm and pointed up. Roy's gaze went above them. The hornet's nests.

"Hold on, Wells," he said as he put his M-16 down. "Let's be reasonable. What can you do now?"

"I can take her out of here and back to her father," He said.

"Thompson said you sent him to kill all of us, including her," said Roy.

"Thompson's a fuck up. Those weren't my orders," Wells shouted.

"From the actions he has been taking and from how you sent him after me, pardon me if I don't quite trust you," said Roy.

Annie looked at Tom, then looked up at the nest and back to Sarah.

While Roy kept Wells occupied, Tom pointed to the nest and signaled Caleb to shoot the nest. Caleb hesitated. Tom whispered, "Shoot it, she will be okay."

Caleb nodded and drew and let the arrow fly. It struck the branch with tremendous force, and the nest dropped directly on Wells's head. He was startled and jumped back, pulling Sarah with him. But then the pain hit him. He was being stung hundreds of times, all in a few moments. He dropped his gun and flailed about, trying to knock the hornets off of him. Sarah simply stepped away from him. Then she hummed a little tune, and the hornets flew up into the tree.

Wells was on the ground, barely holding it together, whimpering in pain. He started to go into shock. He couldn't see and could barely breathe. Soon he was at the edge of being unconscious, yet there was no relief from the pain even then.

Caleb stepped over to Annie and Sarah. He lifted them up onto Gray's back.

"You done good, Gray," Caleb said as he stroked Gray's nose. "Take them back to Sunshine." He handed them the bag of herbs they had gathered and sent them on their way. "Tom make sure they get back and send Frank and Scott down here. We need to decide what to do with this asshole."

Gray took the girls back up the path to the cabins. Tom followed them on foot.

Roy and Caleb stood facing each other. The cold steel eyes were still intimidating, but they no longer frightened Roy. He had a similar look to his own eyes now.

"Do you hear Quinn too?" Roy asked.

Caleb laughed, realizing that he had never heard anyone say the Irishman's name before, but back in the recesses of his shared memories, the name was there. "Yeah, I've spoken to him often." He then extended his hand.

Roy took it in a firm grasp, "My name is Steve Roy. Sorry, our first meeting was less than friendly."

Caleb nodded, "My name is Caleb Teach. I think our first meeting was my fault. That was the first time I remember missing my target," he smiled and continued, "kinda glad I did now."

Zeke rolled to his feet as the two men laughed and swung his gun around, pointing at Caleb's back. Before he pulled the trigger, Roy saw him, pulled Caleb forward forcefully, and stepped in front of the old man. The shot hit him in the chest, and he knew he was done.

He was lung-shot, and he went down hard. Caleb swung through the movement pulling his own weapon, emptying all six shots from his left hand Colt; each bullet hit his target; four into the man's chest and the final two into his face. The shots were so quick that they couldn't have been counted.

Roy was struggling to breathe when Frank and Scott arrived. Scott had Thompson's Sat phone. Scott started first aid on Roy. "You're gonna make it," he said.

Caleb knelt at his side and laid a hand on Scott's, "Let me take care of this. You keep that other'n alive. Frank needs him alive, or these kids will never be safe." Scott was going to protest till he looked into Roy's eyes. Roy nodded and smiled.

Scott stood up and walked over to where Frank was tending to Wells. Wells was in shock—he had been stung more times than either man had ever seen. Scott pulled out his medkit and found the morphine vials. He injected Wells and then started applying the ointments he had to the stings. "I need to get him an epinephrine shot to fight the venom of the stings." He handed Frank the Sat phone. "Call Jamison. We need an extraction team now."

Back at the cabin, Awinita's tea was ready for the final herbs right as the kids came in with the bag; she quickly added them and stirred the mixture while it boiled. Satisfied, she poured it into the mug and took it over to Shashtsoh. She dipped a cloth into the tea and then placed the cloth at his lips, dripping some of the tea into his mouth, just a little at a time. All the while, the Chief and Sunshine had kept the song going. Shashtsoh's eyes fluttered and opened. He saw Awinita over him and smiled as she gave him a few more drops of her tea. She then brought the mug up to his lips. He lifted his head and sipped.

The strength of the tea filled him with warmth, and his color was returning. He turned to the Chief and Sunshine as they finished the song. "Awinita, have you made enough for yourself and them as well?"

Awinita smiled and nodded, "Now you drink more yourself first."

They heard the shots in the woods. The Chief stood. He looked towards the woods, not through the window but directly to where Caleb was as if he could see it all through the wall and trees.

"I must go to them now," he said and strode out the door. He saddled Gray and one of the other horses and led them down the path towards Caleb.

68

The Report

"Sir, Frank Johnston is on the secure line."

"Patch him through, top priority!" Jamison replied. He reached for the phone before it rang and spoke before it got to his head.

"Jamison here," he stated. "Recording started... report."

"Johnston here; I have Wells. He was trying to take the girls. He was going to kill the Langston girl to get the Abraham girl out of here. He sent Thompson out with a team to eliminate us, including our witnesses. We have to do a medical extraction, or we will lose Wells. Transmitting coordinates now from this phone."

"Affirmative, recording ended." Jamison called out to the front, "Send the medivac team and have them follow the coordinates on that Sat phone." He then turned back to the call.

"What about Thompson and his team?"

"Thompson is not going to be a problem going forward. Roy eliminated him," Johnston replied

"I will have to thank him personally when we get you all off that mountain." Jamison waited. There was too long a pause.

"That may not happen; he's been shot. It's not looking good," Johnston said.

Frank turned to look back at Roy and Caleb; they were gone. The Chief was striding over to them. "The Chosen have returned beyond," the Chief said simply in response to Frank's unspoken question. "What can I do to help here?"

Scott cast his gaze about. There was no sign of Roy or Caleb anywhere. "Hornet stings," he said, simply shocked that he had not noticed the others leaving.

The Chief smiled. "I have just the thing." He reached into his bag, pulled out some leaves, and crushed them in his palm. He applied the leaves to the stings and shoved some under Wells' tongue. "He will recover but not too quickly. This man doesn't deserve quick relief." The Chief then turned and strode back up the path towards the cabins.

The Satphone rang. Frank looked at it, but it was not Thompson's phone; it was Wells's. Scott picked it up and gave a short acknowledgment.

"We found the car, sir," came the voice. "It is loaded, and we are ready for your extraction."

"We took some fire," said Scott, "Wells is down. I am bringing him out. All the others are dead—Thompson killed them all. I've already called medivac for Wells. We will meet you at the car. Give me your coordinates. I'll redirect them there."

Frank looked at Scott, "What was that all about?"

Scott smiled. "They didn't hear your report to Jamison. They think you're dead with everyone else and will report that. It will give you time to get those kids out and safe. Follow that Chief. I think he can get you somewhere no one will find you. I'll get this ass-hat down to meet his team. We'll wrap it all up real tidy."

Frank smiled and took off after the Chief. Scott lifted Wells over his shoulder and started hauling him down the path.

69

Safety

Frank passed Scott's plan and the location to Jamison as he went back up the trail. He caught up to the Chief. They and the kids went with Awinita and Shashtsoh deeper into the woods. They returned to the tribe's village—it was like returning in time. They were welcomed as a family returning home for a celebration. In front of their new family, Tom proposed to Sarah. She jumped into his arms and kissed him deeply.

"Yes, what took you so long?" she said.

Everyone laughed and danced. The Chief performed the native ceremony right there in front of the tribe. They celebrated deep into the night.

The following day Frank and Tom had to leave. Frank had called Scott and confirmed that the plan was in place with Jamison. Everyone thought Frank and the kids were dead. Frank and Tom would have to go back to decrypt the remaining documents and stay in a new safe house. They would need to remain hidden and provide testimony in secret. Scott and the remaining men from Thompson's team would corroborate the testimony. Wells might be a problem, but Jamison was sure he could handle the bastard.

70

Jamison and Forrester

The world outside had no idea this building was a medical facility. Two patients were now under guard. Jamison was sitting next to Wells, who was handcuffed to the bed and was recovering slowly. The number of stings he had received should have killed him. Whatever that Chief had given him had worked more effectively than any epinephrine shot they would have used. It would also have been too late by the time they would have been able to administer it.

Wells had just recently awakened; he was startled to find Jamison and Forrester over his bed when he woke. They told him the girls were dead from the same hornets that had attacked him. He knew instantly that he was done—Abraham would be coming for him now. He agreed to testify for his own protection. He caved faster than Jamison had expected. He revealed that Eric Abraham used several people inside the agency to advance his business and political aspirations. Wells admitted he had been instrumental in steering the investigations towards Abraham's competitors. As Abraham moved further up the power chain, he worked to gain political influence. He was trying to eliminate competition through his contacts by using his money and influence to ensure he would be on the ticket for lieutenant governor in the next election. When Sarah was taken, his first concern was not to get her back right away. He was planning to use the kidnapping of his daughter to further his campaign chances and maybe even move to Governor. As they studied the documentation from Tom and Annie's father, they found that Abraham's money and influence had reached all the way up to the current state legislature. The number of people going to be investigated was climbing quickly. The corruption charges in some cases were updated to add the murders that were carried out for Abraham. Some people would be released from prison as they had been convicted on false testimonies Abraham had paid for. They just needed to prove Wells was telling the truth.

Abraham himself provided the proof the following day. He was irate when he was told that everyone at the site was killed, including his daughter. He called Wells' Satphone directly, but this time the phone was answered by Forrester and Jamison. The call was recorded, and this proved to be Abraham's undoing. He spoke before waiting for Wells to speak.

"Wells, you are a dead man! I will have my team hunting you down for the rest of your short life. There will be nowhere you can hide your incompetent ass. You have ruined everything. I told you to kill that fucking investigation. I paid you enough to do it. You said it was done. Well, it came back, and they were getting close again. What the fuck did you do now? You said you had her and were bringing her back!" Mr. Abraham finally paused for breath.

Before he could utter another word, Forrester spoke: "Mr.

Abraham? I regret to inform you that Martin Wells is dead."

There was a pause for a few moments before the phone hung up.

Forrester turned to Jamison, "Was that recorded?"

Ward Jamison smiled, then nodded.

"Good," said Forrester. He picked up his phone, dialed, and ordered the men surveilling Abraham to immediately initiate the arrest. He hung up, trusting his men would perform admirably. "Now, back to your little problem."

Jamison called in his assistant. "Krista, please come into my office."

"Sir," she saluted as she entered and, seeing Forrester, paused a moment before proceeding into the offered chair.

"Miss Lindsay, please state your full name," said Forrester.

"Krista Lindsay, sir," she replied.

"You already acknowledged you were sending documents to Wells," said Jamison.

"Yes, sir," she replied.

"Were your orders direct from Wells?" Forrester asked. "Or do you know if they were from someone else?"

"Sir," she paused before continuing, "I was told the orders came from you. Wells said you had Ward Jamison under investigation. I was to relay only items on this list to Wells." She handed over a list of items to look for in the correspondence going out of the office.

Forrester looked over the list. He handed it to Jamison before speaking again. "Miss Lindsay, I never ordered this. How was this delivered to you?"

"Inner office secure envelope, sir."

"Do you still have the envelope?"

"Yes, sir."

She reached into her bag and pulled out the last two messages. "Here, sir. I did not do anything with these. After I heard about Wells, I turned myself in."

They took the packages from her and held them up for the cameras. Then Forrester opened the first one. It was a request that appeared to be from Forrester's office. He recognized the false watermark and pointed it out to Jamison. It was close, but he had a specific item added to his watermark that was missing from this document. These were authorizations to move Jamison's teams to different investigations and transfer complete control of these investigations to other groups.

"Thank you, Miss Lindsay. You can return to your desk," Jamison said.

"Sir?" She asked incredulously. "You want me to stay?"

"Yes, Miss Lindsay, I imagine you are going to be especially diligent going forward now. I know I can trust you."

"Thank you, Sir!" she stood and stepped back to her desk.

Forrester looked at him. "You sure?"

Jamison nodded. "Absolutely, she only did what her training taught her. She was ordered to take part in an investigation and followed orders related to that investigation." He smiled. "Now she has been exposed to this kind of corruption, she will be that much more diligent and be more aware of what to look for. I will give her further training; I think she will be as good as Johnston before long, and I will get her in the field. She is wasted at that desk out there."

Forrester nodded. "She will have to testify. That may slow your plans to promote her."

Jamison looked at him. "It shouldn't, but if it does, it will just give me more time to train her. So she will be even more ready when it comes."

They continued working late into the night, arranging the documentation for the case. Abraham was being arrested, and they were kept abreast of the developments as they occurred. They continued interviewing Thompson's team one at a time; all were cleared of charges in return for testimony, and they all agreed to testify that Thompson had killed their targets. Carter was the one who made sure all the men knew what to say. All the men reported the same story from different perspectives but close enough that the stories corroborated but not close enough to seem rehearsed. Jamison was disappointed that Roy had been shot. Scott reported directly that he treated the wound himself, knowing it was fatal. There was no way Roy could have survived the trip, even if they had reached the medivac helicopter. Jamison felt that this was the only part of this mission that was a failure. Steve Roy deserved better; from what Scott had stated, Roy had basically foiled Thompson's plan and taken the bastard out by himself. He wished he could have been there for that. He kept the stories of the old man and an American Indian out of his reports—they were too unbelievable to put in. It would throw doubt into the entire case, and he couldn't afford that.

71

Caleb's Choice

Steve Roy was on the Chief's horse climbing the mountain next to Caleb on Gray. Caleb had retold him of the Chosen. His version was slightly different than that told by Quinn but similar enough that he could tell it was just perspective. He knew he would tell it differently as well.

As they climbed the mountain, he also heard the voices in his head. They were constant, and he was building memories of other lives. Lives that were becoming his memories. He was still himself, but now he was more than he was before, and it kept growing larger the further up the mountain they climbed. All the while, Caleb was speaking to him, telling him now of his own story. Steve Roy was amazed but could not dispute the truth of what was happening. Even as Caleb spoke, the memories entered Roy and became part of him. Caleb's memories were becoming his own. He was bewildered, but he had witnessed too much for him to doubt it, not the least of which was looking at the vicious scar on his chest. That hollow point bullet had torn his lung to shreds. He shouldn't be able to breathe now. However, the wound was healed, and the scar tissue already looked a couple of years old. He took another deep breath, amazed there was no pain. Finally, they reached a stream coming down between some trees. As they followed the water, a path next to the creek seemed to open through the trees before them and close off behind them. The voices were getting louder the further they moved up the mountain.

To Caleb, the voices were always there. Caleb knew them and had been listening to them for so long that he had nearly become one with them. He was both excited and sad; he believed he was finally done with his penance and could lay down his life and finally rest. After so long, he looked forward to finally passing from this life into the next. He was excited, but he found he was not nearly as ready as he had believed. His thoughts kept going to Annie, Sarah and Tom. He would miss them, but the voices were reassuring him that he had earned his rest.

At first, the voices spoke to Caleb as he led Steve Roy back to the cave. He was telling Roy the history of the Chosen, as the Irishman had told him—how the choice was given and, if accepted, the mission of the Chosen could not be put aside. As he spoke, the voices had returned to the forefront of his mind. They were helping him now as always, ensuring that he could remember and relay all the history to the next Chosen. As they climbed the mountain, he spoke what the voices instructed him to say. They continued up the path until they came to a clearing and found the cave. Here the voices changed, becoming fewer and fewer in his mind until it was just the voice of the Irishman that he could hear. Caleb did not realize he had stopped speaking as they rode.

Steve Roy had been listening to Caleb speak, all the while

hearing the exact words Caleb was saying but in that other voice, the voice that called him Buachaill. As they had ridden, the other voices were growing in his mind filling him with knowledge and experiences that were not his own. As they reached a small clearing, he saw the cave next to a small stream that ran away from a spring on the side of the mountain. It was then that he realized it was not Caleb speaking to him. He was listening to many voices but could still hear the Irish voice. Now that voice was talking to Caleb.

"Caleb, there is a new choice before you. This man is to be the Chosen now; he has made his choice; however, something new has occurred in his choosing. He made his choice before he was mortally wounded. He chose to serve this role while he was yet still living. This act gives you a new choice to make."

"What choice?" Caleb asked.

"If you so choose, you can remain as Chosen with Steve Roy or become a guide to him as I have been with you. You may choose to remain in this world now to live out the remainder of your life here in this time. But, you also may choose to be reborn and live a new life in this new world that you have helped to protect all these years."

Caleb looked at Steve, then looked back to the cave. "What of you? Would that not extend your penance beyond your time?"

The Irishman laughed, "Ná bíodh imní ort, I am in my paradise; I am a member of the voices. I will not be troubled to stay in this role and will be available to the Chosen for all times. That was my choice, and it suits me. You may make this choice granted to you by this man's sacrifice."

Steve heard this exchange; he spoke then: "Caleb, I am grateful to have met you and to have both fought against you and beside you. I would be proud to serve with you, but you've earned this choice. I will see you again regardless of where you choose to go."

Caleb smiled, his face softened, and his eyes shone. "Roy, let's get settled. You'll know what choice I make when I choose it." He showed Roy into the cave and stowed his gear and weapons. Roy marveled as the roots wrapped around and protected them. All the while, Caleb was telling him more of the history; he then led him back outside. Caleb took the saddle, blanket, and bridle off Gray, wrapped the tackle in the blanket, and tucked it under the saddle as he placed it back in the cave. Caleb then went back to Gray and turned him towards the path down the mountain stroking Gray's neck and nose.

"Gray, you have been a fine companion," Caleb said as he stroked Gray's snout. "I am glad she found your name. I would never have known you fully if she hadn't. You are free now, Gray, forever. You choose your own path now. Go and live the life you choose."

Caleb stepped back; Gray followed a step, nuzzled Caleb for a moment, then turned and slowly walked out of the clearing. Caleb gave him a parting pat on the rump as he passed.

Steve had removed the saddle and bridle of the other horse, using new knowledge, memories that were not his own but were still his. He had stored the gear and stepped out to hear Gray's parting words to Caleb. Roy's horse nickered, then followed Gray down the mountain.

The men then turned back towards the cave. Steve Roy extended his hand. "Thank you, Caleb; you have made my life worthwhile again."

Caleb took his hand and smiled again, "Roy, I know I will

see you again."

Caleb gestured for Steve to enter ahead of him. As Steve stepped through the entrance, he heard a sound behind him that seemed like a flock of birds taking flight. He smiled, then turned back to find Caleb was gone. There was no trace of him having been there. Steve placed the remainder of his equipment on the rock shelves in the cave, still smiling. "Yes, we will see each other again," he muttered. He had felt what Caleb's choice was the moment it was made.

"Good choice Caleb," he said out loud. He then lay down on the flat rock deep in the cave and let the sleep take him. He realized the cave mouth was closing even as he was falling asleep. He realized he was no longer breathing. Most men would have been fearful, but he was calm. He knew it would not be long before he was called back in this world.

"Yes, Buachaill, you will be called back luath go leor."

Gray followed the path down the mountain. He came to a clearing and turned to look back up the mountain. The other horse paused, waiting for him to lead on. There was no path behind them. The horse following him down off the mountain just stood still, waiting for him to choose their direction. Gray turned and looked out over the plains. There he saw a herd of wild horses and his heart leaped; he yearned to follow the mountain down there and take that herd as his own. That feeling was so strong that he actually began to step that way for several yards before stopping. He turned back and looked in the other direction. His other herd was back there—the herd of young people that he would need to protect. The girl was back there too. He turned around to look at the wild horses running across the land below one more time. He hesitated a few minutes before turning away from the plains. The other horse nodded its head and followed Gray as he headed back to the girl.

72

Epilogue

Almost a year later, the investigation was still ongoing. The lawyers had argued vehemently. The questioning had been tough and draining, but Ward Jamison had prevailed. Due to his testimony and Scott, Carter, and Carter's men, Frank Johnston would be remembered as a hero. To the world, Frank Johnston had died in the line of duty. He had given everything trying to protect them but could not save the kids.

The official documents state that Frank singlehandedly protected the kids as long as any lone man could. But Thomas, Annie, and Sarah were gone. There were just too many men attacking them for one man to defend them.

The evidence found at the site and the documentation Frank had turned in previously had exposed and led to the arrest of several politicians and many prominent businessmen. The most important one caught was Eric Abraham. He was a broken man now and faced charges of corruption and several acts of collusion that led to the deaths of the entire Langston family, his own daughter Sarah Abraham, the old woman named Maribel, and several others.

Ward Jamison studied more documents, knowing it was up to him to redeem the image of the whole office. Forrester had been promoted up two levels and had brought Jamison along with him. They were now cleaning house. Jamison was still angry about the whole mess. He had handled the situation by the book, but the book had failed him. He would now rewrite it and change what needed to be changed. This was now his watch, and his new team would not lose any of their charges again. To the world, his department had failed on a level from which it would be difficult to recover. It was now up to him to do so. He would make sure Tom and the girls would be remembered as the last charges his department lost.

No one would know that Tom and Frank had been secluded in a very secure location with a computer room tied directly to the internet behind a special set of firewalls. They had been exposing more and more of the corruption. Abraham's influence had been followed to the federal level, where even the Vice President's office had been shocked to find colleagues were being arrested.

The Vice President had looked at the evidence on his desk, proving that his own staff had been involved. He had tendered his resignation, but the President was delaying accepting it—knowing he was not truly involved. The President would protect him as long as he could.

Ward had handled the most challenging task himself, telling the Abraham family of the loss of Sarah. It had been horrible for them, mainly because her father, Eric Abraham, had been the cause. Jamison wished he could tell them she was okay, but no one could ever know she survived. There were just too many still out there who would try to exact revenge. This had become evident when Martin Wells was found in his cell. There was not a mark on him, but he was dead. Someone had got to him even in the secure holding cell. Although some of the guards reported that Wells kept complaining that he heard buzzing from a hornet's nest, he was the only one who ever heard them, and no nest was ever found.

Tom and Frank worked to decrypt all of the documents in the recovered data. This was the only way to put an end to this. They both needed to remain 'dead' to the outside world to do so and remain safe. Only Forrester and Jamison knew they were alive, and only Jamison knew where they were. They were reporting only to Ward Jamison. No one on Jamison's team even knew where Jamison acquired the data he was delivering.

Ward checked his messages at his desk. "Time to get to work," he said aloud to no one in particular. He sat back down and grabbed his phone. "Miss Lindsay, please report to my office."

Several months later, Sarah happily chatted about silly things with Annie behind the cabin. The Chief smiled at Shashtsoh—they had accepted the girls and the boy as family. They were like a pair of proud Grandparents. Sunshine and Awinita were teaching the girls their ways. The girls were becoming great healers beneath their tutelage, and Annie's skills as a prophet grew.

They had been waiting for a long time for the promised return of Tom and Frank. When they finally returned, the Chief and Shashtsoh together hoped to preserve and pass on the knowledge to them before the Chief was gone. His ancestors accepted the young people, and the Chief would keep them safe with his family. No one would ever notice them there with the Chiefs family. In fact, no one ever looked in on the reservation's people too closely. And he could keep them safe and hidden. He looked out again at his new granddaughters and smiled.

Sarah was holding her baby. This was her miracle baby; he had healed her heartache after finding out about her father and learning she would never be able to see her family again. This little man was the love of her life. He had been born early, only seven months after the ordeal. But he was strong and healthy. He had jet black hair and cute little dimples like Thomas. His eyes were the most starling pale gray that seemed as though he could look through you into your soul. Annie said they were just like Caleb's eyes. Sarah agreed and named him Caleb Thomas. He was a very alert baby; he rarely fussed and seemed to enjoy being alive. He loved watching Annie and Sarah care for the horses. Gray would lean against Annie and nuzzle her, looking for apples and carrots. He would also come and gently nuzzle little Caleb Thomas from time to time as if to say thank you.

Suddenly Gray's ears twitched, and he nuzzled Annie's shoulder. He shook his head when she looked up at him, then turned and stomped. Annie knew someone was coming and reached out with her feelings. She smiled and looked at Sarah and little Caleb when she realized who was coming. She didn't want to miss this reunion. Sarah caught her look and frowned, trying to figure out why Annie was looking at her like that. She turned back in time to see Tom and Frank stepping out of the trees. Her heart leaped, and she scooped up little Caleb and took him to meet his father.

www.ingramcontent.com/pod-product-compliance
Lightning Source LLC
LaVergne TN
LVHW010541160826
845677LV00013B/2958

* 9 7 9 8 3 6 1 8 7 7 8 2 9 *